D0597243

The Wishing Wings
Tiger Streak's Tale
Blue Rain's Adventure

The Butterfly Wishes series
The Wishing Wings
Tiger Streak's Tale
Blue Rain's Adventure
Spring Shine Sparkles

Butterfly Wishes

Jennifer Castle

illustrated by Tracy Bishop

The Wishing Wings

Tiger Streak's Tale

Blue Rain's Adventure

BLOOMSBURY

NEW YORK   LONDON   OXFORD   NEW DELHI   SYDNEY

The Wishing Wings and Tiger Streak's Tale first published in the United States of America in 2017
Blue Rain's Adventure first published in the United States of America in April 2018
by Bloomsbury Children's Books
Bind-up published in the United States of America in April 2018
www.bloomsbury.com

Bloomsbury is a registered trademark of Bloomsbury Publishing Plc

For information about permission to reproduce selections from this book, write to
Permissions, Bloomsbury Children's Books, 1385 Broadway, New York, New York 10018
Bloomsbury books may be purchased for business or promotional use. For information on
bulk purchases please contact Macmillan Corporate and Premium Sales Department at
specialmarkets@macmillan.com

Library of Congress Cataloging-in-Publication Data
for each title is available upon request
The Wishing Wings LCCN: 2017007247
Tiger Streak's Tale LCCN: 2017007281
Blue Rain's Adventure LCCN: 2017021642

ISBN 978-1-5476-0043-4 (bind-up)

Typeset by Westchester Publishing Services
Printed and bound in the U.S.A. by Berryville Graphics Inc., Berryville, Virginia
2 4 6 8 10 9 7 5 3 1

All papers used by Bloomsbury Publishing, Inc., are natural, recyclable products
made from wood grown in well-managed forests. The manufacturing processes
conform to the environmental regulations of the country of origin.

The Wishing Wings and *Tiger Streak's Tale*

For S. and C.,
the butterfly spirits in my life

Blue Rain's Adventure

For Erica Chase-Salerno,
butterfly spirit extraordinaire

Butterfly Wishes

Wishes

The Wishing Wings

PROLOGUE

The sun scattered gleaming streaks of light through a grove of willow trees. Two butterflies flitted in and out of the rays, riding the breeze toward one tree that was taller and thicker than the others.

In the center of this tree was a deep hollow covered with a carpet of shaggy moss. The butterflies landed softly on it.

"Do you see, Mama?" said one butterfly as she climbed to the top of the hollow. In a neat row hung four gray shapes. Each one was a chrysalis, a small, hard bubble inside which a caterpillar was changing into a butterfly. "The chrysalides should be gold," added the butterfly, "but they're not!"

This butterfly's wings were colored pink and turquoise, with cloud-shaped patterns on them. Now she flapped those wings nervously, hovering around the four chrysalides.

"Yes, Sky Dance," the other butterfly said with an echo of worry. "I do see. They should be lighting up, too." She was bigger, splashed with shades of brilliant red, forest green, and shining silver. The colors made a pattern that looked like a

rose on each wing. She was Queen Rose Glow.

Sky Dance landed next to her mother. "Something's very wrong," she said, her voice shaking.

"I feel it, too," murmured Rose Glow. "These New Blooms are surely under a dark enchantment. Who knows what they'll be like when they emerge? If they can't grant someone a wish by sunset on their first day . . ."

". . . they'll lose their magic," finished Sky Dance. The thought of it made her shudder.

One chrysalis was wiggling a bit. Almost dancing. Mother and daughter stared at it with extra love and excitement in their eyes. It was special to them.

"Your sister will have her new wings before the sun breaks over that hill," said Rose Glow.

"I can't wait to see her!" Sky Dance exclaimed, but then she got serious again. "But, Mama," she added, "who would put such a curse on the New Blooms?"

Rose Glow's huge eyes grew darker. "Someone who wants to steal their magic for themselves," she said. "If the New Blooms lose their magic, we all lose a little magic, too. Our magic might even get so weak that it disappears completely." Rose Glow touched a wing to one of Sky Dance's wings and added, "The time has come for you to seek help on the far side of the meadow."

Sky Dance knew what that meant. It frightened her, but she didn't let it show.

The chrysalis shook harder. As it began to slowly split open, both butterflies took a breath and filled their hearts with hope.

CHAPTER ONE

Addie Gibson lay on the floor of her new bedroom, surrounded by boxes. She rested her head on one labeled Books, which was not at all comfortable, but it felt good to take a break from unpacking.

She stared out the window, where all she could see was blue sky and the corner of one puffy cloud. *What is Violet doing right now?* Addie wondered, running her fingers over the woven bracelet on her wrist and thinking of her best friend. *Does the sky look the same out her window?* It had only been three days since Addie's family moved from the city to Brook Forest, but she already missed Violet so much that it hurt.

Suddenly, the bedroom door burst open and there stood Clara, Addie's younger sister. She clutched a stuffed orange cat under one arm.

"I can't find my pencils and sketch pads," Clara announced angrily. "Do you have them?"

"I don't know," replied Addie. "I just opened a box of art supplies. Look over

there." She pointed to a big box in the corner.

Clara marched over to the box and looked inside, then pulled out a set of colored pencils. "Aha! You *did* take them!"

"I did not!" Addie snapped back. "The movers must have packed up our stuff together."

Addie heard the jingle of a collar. Her little black-and-white dog, Pepper, scurried into the room and jumped into Addie's arms.

Clara looked at Addie and the dog with a frown. She asked, "Why does Pepper always take your side? He likes you better, and it's not fair. I've been begging Mom and Dad for my own dog for ages!"

The girls' mother appeared in the doorway behind Clara and clapped her hands. "Both of you, hush," she commanded. "You haven't stopped fighting since we first walked into this house!"

Clara gave her mother a furious look, then gave Addie a *super* furious look, and stomped off. They heard her bedroom door slam.

Mom sighed, then said to Addie, "Forgive your sister. She's really sad about the move."

"She must be," added Addie, "if she's walking around hugging Squish." Squish was the name of Clara's stuffed cat, her favorite toy since she was a baby.

Mom nodded. "Brook Forest is so different from the city. I know it's a big change. Are you sad, too?"

Addie buried her face in the scruff of Pepper's neck. "I'm okay," she said. It wasn't completely true. She *was* sad, but she was trying hard not to be.

"Everything will be better once we're settled in," Mom reassured her. "It won't seem so different anymore, and you'll both make new friends. Why don't you take Pepper outside while I help your sister calm down?"

"Outside?" asked Addie.

Her mother laughed. "Yes, honey. We have a backyard now. You should be exploring it."

"But there's nature out there! Dirt and leaves and bugs and . . . flying things."

"Isn't it wonderful?" Mom said with a smile. "Catch one of them, then bring it back for us to see."

❦ ❦ ❦

Pepper tugged hard at his leash, pulling Addie from the house onto the back deck, and then onto the grass.

"Okay, okay!" she grumbled at her dog. "I get it! You like it out here. That makes one of us."

Truth was, Addie *did* like her yard. She just didn't like the woods that lay beyond it. The stretch of grass behind the house ended at a line of identical trees that made a kind of fence. All Addie could see on the other side of them were more trees, branches, and leaves. It was as if they went on forever. She could hear strange noises, too. Her parents said it was only birds chirping and squirrels scampering, just like in the park near their old apartment, but here they sounded extra-spooky.

Suddenly, there were giggling voices nearby. Addie peered across some bushes to the house next door and glimpsed the top of a swing set. Maybe she would meet the neighbor kids soon. The thought of it made her stomach do a flip-flop.

The kids started shouting at one another, and Addie tried to hear what they were saying. She was listening so hard, she didn't realize she'd loosened her grip on Pepper's leash . . .

Just like that, Pepper was off running, chasing a squirrel toward the row of trees.

"No!" yelled Addie after him, but he shot like a rocket past the trees and into the woods, disappearing almost instantly. "Pepper!" she yelled. "Come back!"

Addie was quiet for a moment, listening for signs of her dog. Out of the corner of her eye, something bright flitted in the distance. When she turned to look, it was gone.

"Pepper!" Addie hollered. "You bad, bad boy!"

There was no time to get help. Pepper was fast. The longer Addie waited to go after him, the farther away he might get.

"Be brave," she said to herself, and took the longest, deepest, courage-creating breath she could.

Addie stepped through the trees, then paused. *This isn't so bad*, she thought. Just a little cooler and darker. Only a little scary.

She took another step, then another. By the third step, she was officially in the woods now . . . and she felt okay!

Addie started running, calling Pepper's name. Somewhere nearby, she could hear the faint jingle of his collar. Her sneakers kicked rocks as she ran, and leaves scratched her bare legs. She ducked under a low branch to avoid smashing into it, but lost her balance and tripped on a thick tree root. Addie barely had time to put out her hands to break her fall.

"Ouch!" she cried as she hit the dirt. She lay there for a second, then slowly stood up, examining her arms and legs to see if she was hurt.

She wasn't, but now she was definitely lost. She brushed herself off, then turned in a circle to see if she could spot a house somewhere. Nothing. There were just woods, woods, and more woods.

"Pepper!" she yelled. "Mom! Clara!"

Nobody answered.

Addie sat down on the ground and hugged her knees to her chest. "You're not scared," she said aloud to herself. "You're fine. Your house is probably on the other side of those trees."

Suddenly, something fluttered past her. Addie saw flashes of pink and turquoise.

Then Pepper emerged from a bush, chasing after it.

🦋 🦋 🦋

Addie followed Pepper's little white-tipped tail into a clearing.

"Pepper, stop!" she commanded. "Leave that butterfly alone!"

Suddenly, the butterfly slowed down, flitting in circles above Pepper's head.

Pepper started running in circles, too. It gave Addie a chance to catch up to him and grab the leash.

"Got you!" she exclaimed once she had it firmly in her hands.

That was strange, Addie thought. It was almost as if the butterfly had done that on purpose, to help her.

Pepper barked at the butterfly, who was still hovering close to them. It darted up and down, back and forth. Addie didn't want Pepper to hurt it.

"Best to tie you up so I can chase this poor thing away," Addie told the dog. She looped his leash around the trunk of a small tree. Once Pepper realized he wasn't going anywhere, he lay down in the grass and put his chin on his paws, panting.

Then Addie turned to the butterfly. "That stinker won't bother you anymore," she said. "Go! Be free!"

But the butterfly didn't leave. It flew even lower. Addie could hear its wings flapping. She could feel the little breeze it made as it flitted by her head. What was it doing?

Maybe it wants to play, thought Addie for a second. But no, that would be ridiculous. Right?

Still, the butterfly did seem very interested in her. Addie was also very interested in *it*. Now that she could get a better look, Addie thought it was the most beautiful and unusual butterfly she'd ever seen. The colors on its wings were so bright, and the pattern on them almost looked like clouds. How strange!

She remembered what her mother said about exploring and catching something. Before she knew it, Addie was reaching out her hands toward the butterfly. It floated above them as if making up its mind, then landed gently, with a tiny tickle, on one of Addie's palms.

Addie carefully cupped her other palm over the butterfly and peered into the little house she'd made with her hands. She'd never been this close to one before. The butterfly slowly flapped its wings, maybe tired out from all that flying. Its antennae stood straight at attention, and it appeared to be looking right back at her with a furry pink face and dark, bead-shaped eyes.

"Hello there," said Addie.

"Hello to you, too," said the butterfly in a voice as high and clear as bells ringing.

Addie was so surprised, she stumbled backward into the dirt again.

CHAPTER TWO

Addie sat up and looked around for the person who'd said hello to her. Nobody was there except for Pepper, who was already snoozing in the sun.

"Who said that?" Addie called out.

The butterfly had escaped Addie's hands when she fell. Now it was zigzagging around her. After a moment, it landed daintily on her knee and said, in that same musical voice, "I did!"

Addie stared at it and blinked twice. Was she imagining this? Had she hit her head?

"You're a butterfly," said Addie. "Butterflies don't talk."

"I'm a Wishing Wing," replied the butterfly matter-of-factly. "And Wishing Wings *do* talk. When we have something to say, of course. We don't go around chattering for no reason. My name's Sky Dance, and I need your help!"

"I'm Addie." Addie was still not sure this was really happening. "What's a Wishing Wing?"

Sky Dance's wings quivered. "We don't have much time," she said anxiously, "but I suppose I should explain a few things first." She was silent for a few moments, her little head tilted as if she were thinking. "Okay," the butterfly continued. "Have you ever suddenly felt like you wanted to take off running because you were so happy? Have you ever started dancing and singing for no reason?"

Addie thought about that. "Yes," she replied. "Not lately, but yes."

"Have you ever felt really strong, like you could do anything you put your mind to?"

"Sometimes," muttered Addie. It had been a while in that department, too.

"That's because of us!" exclaimed Sky Dance, shooting into the air and flying around Addie's head. "That's the power of the Wishing Wing butterflies! Regular butterflies spread pollen. We spread the butterfly spirit . . . by granting wishes. We're magic!"

"Magic . . ." Addie echoed. It was one of her favorite words. "I love magic. Too bad this is just a dream."

"You're not dreaming!" Sky Dance said in a frustrated voice. She landed on Addie's other knee and moved her wings in quick, short flaps. "I'll prove it to you."

"How?"

"By granting you a wish, silly!" Sky Dance suddenly lowered her voice, more serious now. "But you get just one. Every human child gets one. There's only so much magic to go around, you know, so you must choose carefully. What is the thing you want most in the world right now?"

Addie thought about the question. It was a tough one! Nobody had ever asked her that before. She knew she was supposed to name something like a pony or a trillion dollars. But when she closed her eyes and concentrated on what would make her happiest at that moment, the first image that popped into her head was Violet's face. Addie found herself reaching for the bracelet on her wrist—the one that Violet had made for her as a good-bye gift.

Before she knew it, Addie was saying, "I wish my best friend Violet and I could stay close forever, even though we live far apart now."

Sky Dance flitted over to Addie's wrist and examined the bracelet. "Violet must be special to you," she said.

"She is. Missing her is the worst thing about moving to Brook Forest."

"Okay, then!" proclaimed Sky Dance. "I can fix that. Hold out your arm."

Addie did as she was told. Sky Dance paused for a moment, then flew a quick circle around Addie's wrist. She left a trail of colors behind her, a striped rainbow with the dazzling pink, turquoise, and white of her wings.

She flew a second time around Addie's wrist . . . and then a third.

When she was done, Sky Dance landed back on Addie's knee. The rainbow she'd made hung in the air, sparkling like fireworks. When it faded, Addie looked at her arm and gasped in surprise.

The woven bracelet had been transformed into a gleaming gold chain. A heart-shaped locket dangled from the center of it.

"Open it!" said Sky Dance, sounding very pleased with herself.

Addie opened the locket. Inside was a picture of her and Violet together, hugging and smiling at the camera. It was a photo Addie's mother had taken at Addie's last birthday party. Addie was suddenly overcome with the feeling that Violet was with her.

"What . . . How did you . . . When . . ." Addie simply could not find words for this situation.

Sky Dance laughed. "That's Wishing Wing magic for you. It's powerful stuff! I put some extra in the locket. It'll keep your friendship with Violet strong."

"Whoa," muttered Addie, touching the smooth surface of the locket. It was so shiny, she could see her reflection in it. "I love this. Thank you!"

She reached out to hug Sky Dance, then realized that . . . well . . . she couldn't really hug a butterfly. Instead, she put out her finger and Sky Dance landed on it. Addie brought Sky Dance close to her face, and they stared into each other's eyes.

"I guess seeing is believing," Addie said after a moment. "You *are* real."

"Yes, indeed. So you'll help us?"

"What's the trouble, exactly?"

Sky Dance became very still and sighed. "I'm in charge of four New Blooms. That's what we call a Wishing Wing that's just come out of its chrysalis. You know what a chrysalis is, right?"

Addie nodded. "When a caterpillar's ready to turn into a butterfly, it makes a

little house around itself where it does all the changing." She'd seen pictures of them in books, but never one in real life.

"A New Bloom has to earn its magic," continued Sky Dance, "by granting a wish to a human child before sunset. If the New Bloom can't do that, its magic is gone forever! It loses all its colors and its wings become plain white."

"Oh," said Addie softly. "How sad."

Sky Dance folded up her wings so they looked like a single wing, making her look quite solemn. "My sister is one of these New Blooms," she explained. "Someone cast an enchantment on the four chrysalides, but we don't know who or why they'd want to do this. My sister doesn't even realize she's a butterfly. She's confused and afraid. She has to find a human child who needs a wish granted, but she won't leave the Changing Tree!"

"That sounds bad," said Addie. "But why do you think I can help?"

"You can. I had been following you for a little while, but wasn't sure at first if you could help. Then I saw you overcome your fear of the woods by telling yourself to be brave, and I knew you were the one."

It felt strange to Addie—that Sky Dance believed in her like this—but it was a good strange.

"What can I do?" she asked.

"Come with me to Wishing Wing Grove. It's right over there, on the other side of this meadow." Sky Dance began to speak faster as she got more excited. "I'll show you the chrysalides and the Changing Tree! You can meet my parents, too! Then you can help us find a child who needs a wish!"

It did sound wonderful. Still, like with every time she'd faced something new and unfamiliar, Addie couldn't help feeling the tiniest bit afraid.

"What about Pepper?" asked Addie, looking over at her dog. He was still fast asleep.

"Pepper will be fine," assured Sky Dance. "This is Silk Meadow, the entrance to our world. I'll ask a couple of other Wishing Wings to stand guard over him."

Addie and Sky Dance stared at each other for a moment. Addie realized she was on the brink of something amazing. Butterflies! Magic! An adventure! How could she say no?

"Show me the way," said Addie. Now her voice sounded as excited as Sky Dance's.

"Good answer!" laughed Sky Dance, and she took to the air.

Addie began walking quickly after her. She watched Sky Dance zipping and zooming along the breeze. *It's hard to march after a butterfly*, she thought. *It just doesn't feel right.* Addie picked up her pace. She skipped once. Then twice. Sky Dance seemed to be skipping, too, as she flew, and Addie remembered what Sky Dance had said about the butterfly spirit.

Addie sensed it now, in every part of her. She was not sad or shy or scared anymore. She felt *free*.

When Sky Dance sped up, Addie broke into a run alongside her new friend.

CHAPTER THREE

W hen they reached a thicket of
trees at the far side of the
meadow, Sky Dance landed on a low
branch. Addie caught up with her, then
stopped to catch her breath.

"We're here," said Sky Dance proudly.
"Welcome to Wishing Wing Grove!"

Addie stepped into the shade of the

trees and looked around. She saw rocks covered with bright lime-colored moss. Flowers and cattails dotted the grass. Willow trees dangled their leaves like curtains. A cool mist swirled in the air, and Addie could hear the babbling of a nearby creek.

"It's beautiful," sighed Addie.

Two Wishing Wings landed next to Sky Dance. Sky Dance whispered something to them and they flew off toward the spot where Addie knew Pepper lay, hopefully still sleeping.

"Time to meet my parents," proclaimed Sky Dance. "Follow me!"

Addie walked a step behind Sky Dance as they moved deeper into the grove. The air smelled sweet. *Like juice*, thought Addie, *mixed with candy and Mom's perfume.* She slowly breathed it all in, then out.

"Try not to be nervous," said Sky Dance. "They may be queen and king, but they're just Mama and Papa to me, and they're great."

Addie stopped short. "Queen and king?"

Sky Dance chuckled. "Oops! I forgot to tell you! My family are the rulers of Wishing Wing Grove."

"That makes you . . ."

"A princess?" Sky Dance giggled and lowered her voice to a whisper. "Yes, but I don't like to call myself that. I want to be known for being *me*, not just royalty. Even though I'll be queen someday."

Addie was about to ask Sky Dance how she felt about that, but then they came upon a giant boulder. The boulder was covered in a quilt of dazzling colors so lovely it made Addie gasp. It took her a moment to realize the quilt was not made with fabric but with Wishing Wing butterflies. Dozens and dozens of them! Each one's wings were a different pattern of colors and shapes.

"Sky Dance has returned!" Addie heard a voice shout, and a cheer went up among the butterflies. Sky Dance flitted over to the rock, and the crowd made space for her. She landed in front of two butterflies sitting on a ledge at the very top.

Addie hung back, but Sky Dance called out, "Addie! Come closer!"

Addie stepped up to the rock and bowed her head shyly. How do you greet royal butterflies? It wasn't exactly something she'd thought about before. "It's a pleasure to meet you," she finally said.

"Likewise," said one of the two butterflies, bowing her head in return. Addie admired the rose patterns on her red, green, and silver wings. "I am Queen Rose Glow, and we're so happy you've come. We've all been meeting to discuss the enchantment and what it might mean."

"They call me King Flit Flash," said the other butterfly in a low, wise-sounding voice. The king's wings were deep blue and jet black, with white lightning bolts on them. "It's a Wishing Wing's job to help humans, but I've always known that someday we might be the ones who need help. You must be very special if Sky Dance has chosen you."

"Thank you," said Addie, blushing a bit.

"No, thank *you*. How can we ever show our gratitude?" asked Rose Glow.

Flit Flash chuckled. "I have a notion." He whispered something to the queen.

"Excellent idea," she agreed. "Addie will be better able to help us if she can see things the way we see them, even if just for a few minutes." Rose Glow turned back to Addie, who was feeling extremely confused . . . and curious. "Addie, have you ever wanted to be a butterfly?"

"Of course!" she burst out. "Who hasn't?"

Sky Dance gasped. "Mama! Are you going to do what I think you're going to do?"

Rose Glow took to the air and hovered over Sky Dance. "Yes. I'd like you to do it with me. You've been studying how, right?"

"Practicing, too!" shouted Sky Dance. She flew up to meet her mother, then turned to Addie. "Stand very still, okay?"

"Okay," said Addie, not sure if she should be excited or nervous. Right then, she was both.

Rose Glow and Sky Dance flew close to each other and touched their wings together. A brilliant rainbow of pink, turquoise, white, red, green, and silver burst from their wings—both butterflies' colors combined. As they flew side by side around Addie, the rainbow wrapped her like a ribbon. They circled once, twice, three times. Then the colors dissolved into a cloud of glitter.

Suddenly, everything looked different.

Addie was no longer gazing down at the rock. She was peering up at it. Sky Dance and Rose Glow landed next to her, but now they looked bigger.

Wait a minute, thought Addie. *I'm the one who changed! I'm BUTTERFLY-SIZE!*

"Stretch out your wings!" instructed Sky Dance.

Addie stretched out what felt like her arms and glanced to her right.

Instead of her arm, there was a wing. She glanced to her left. Another wing. They were magenta and powder blue.

"Oh my gosh!" exclaimed Addie. "My favorite colors!"

"You must be all heart, my girl," said the queen, pointing an antenna at the lavender heart pattern on her wings. "Now the two of you, fly off. This is rare and powerful magic that only two members of the Wishing Wing royal family can make together, but it lasts just a few minutes."

"Come on, Addie!" said Sky Dance. "On the way to the Changing Tree, I'll show you the rest of the grove."

"But I've never flown before!" Addie protested.

"Maybe not like this. But you've imagined it, right? Just imagine it again!"

Addie closed her eyes and thought about all the flying dreams she'd ever had. She flapped her wings like she did in those dreams . . . and was suddenly in the air. It felt as natural as running!

She heard the *flit-flut* of her wings' silk against the breeze as she went higher. The rocks in the grove looked like mountains. The trees looked like skyscrapers. It was weird, but wonderful, to be so weightless. Addie felt all her worries fall far below her to the ground, and she laughed harder than she had in a long time.

Sky Dance flew up beside her and laughed, too. "Now you've really got the butterfly spirit! Follow me!"

They rose above the boulder, then

fluttered farther into the grove. Soon they were looking down on the creek. The water was crystal clear and Addie could see right through to the blue-green of the creek bottom. On the banks, a cluster of bright yellow crickets jumped through the grass.

"We share the grove with them," called Sky Dance. "We keep them safe, and they help us manage the grove. They play great music, too."

Sky Dance led Addie lower to the ground now, until they both landed on the sprawling roots of a huge oak

tree. There was a hole at the base of the tree. A large red ladybug with yellow spots waddled toward it, carrying a basket of leaves on its back.

"The caterpillar nursery's in here," said Sky Dance. "Come on."

Addie followed Sky Dance into the hole. Inside the tree, dozens of caterpillars of various sizes and every possible color crawled around, munching on leaves. More ladybugs with yellow spots rushed around, frantic to feed the caterpillars as they gobbled up whatever was put in front of them.

"They just eat and grow and eat and grow. Being here brings back some good memories," sighed Sky Dance. "When they're ready to spin their chrysalides, the crickets bring them to the Changing Tree."

After they left the nursery, Sky Dance and Addie came upon a long, thin, bright-green caterpillar with tiny red spikes up and down its back.

"Oh!" Sky Dance gasped in surprise. "Hello, Madame Furia."

"Busy day! Busy day!" said Madame Furia sweetly with a giant smile. One of the caterpillar's red eyeballs looked up while the other looked down toward Addie. "I heard about your new friend. Is this her? She makes a stunning butterfly! Sky Dance, you're beautiful too, of course. And so brave! The both of you!"

"Thank you," said Sky Dance.

Madame Furia grinned again, even wider. "I must be off! The queen has asked me to interview our cricket companions to see what they know about the enchantment."

They watched Madame Furia inch away in the opposite direction.

Sky Dance asked, "Isn't she nice? It's so sad, what happened to her. She was Mama's best friend, back when they were caterpillars. But she broke the rules of the grove, and as punishment, she wasn't allowed to change into a Wishing Wing. She'll stay a caterpillar forever."

"Wow," said Addie. "What did she do that was so bad?"

"Madame Furia thought another caterpillar was trying to steal Mama away as a friend, and got jealous. She made it look like the caterpillar was stealing food from the others so she'd get in trouble, but Furia was the one who got caught in her lies. Mama forgave her. She says everyone makes mistakes sometimes. Now she's in charge of the crickets."

Addie was about to ask Sky Dance to tell her more about these "rules of the grove," but she started to feel a strange, tingly feeling in her arms . . . or rather, her wings. The rainbow suddenly reappeared, spinning around her. Before Addie knew it, she was human-size again. She checked her body, which seemed so big and heavy now, but everything looked in order.

Sky Dance flitted into her field of

vision. "I guess the magic really does only last a few minutes. How do you feel?"

"Like myself. A little sad not to be a butterfly anymore."

"Well, maybe it won't be the last time," said Sky Dance. "Look, we're here at the Changing Tree."

It was an enormous willow, with a thick trunk and branches that curved in all directions. The leaves looked green at first, but when the wind swished and moved them, they turned purple.

Sky Dance flew up to a hollow in the center of the tree's trunk. Addie drew nearer and took a good look at the chrysalides, which instantly filled her with a sense of sadness and that something was very wrong. They hung gray and still as stones. She counted three. The fourth was just an empty shell, crumpled like a gum wrapper.

"I see what you mean," said Addie. "I'm not a Wishing Wing, but even I can feel the dark magic here. But who? And why?"

"We don't know," replied Sky Dance. "One New Bloom will come out each day. My sister was the first. If we can make sure all four of them grant their wishes in time, maybe then the enchantment will be broken and we can figure out who's behind it all."

"Who's down there?" shouted a high, terrified voice from above. "Whoever it is, go away!"

Addie looked up to a nearby branch of the Changing Tree. There sat a butterfly with wings of purple, peach, and mint green, with leaf patterns on them. The wings glistened in the sun because they were not quite dry.

Sky Dance stared up at this butterfly and her eyes glistened, too, but with tears.

"And that," said Sky Dance softly, her voice quivering, "is my sister Shimmer Leaf."

CHAPTER FOUR

From the tips of her antennae to the bottom edges of her wings, Shimmer Leaf's entire body was shaking with fear.

Addie hated being frightened, but not as much as she hated seeing other creatures scared. She put on a big, warm smile and tried to make her voice as soft and soothing as possible. "Hi, Shimmer Leaf. I'm Addie."

Shimmer Leaf peered down at her, then jumped back and squealed. "You're huge!" she cried. "You're a monster!"

Addie tried not to take that personally. She kept smiling. "I'm just human. I'm also a friend, who's here to help you."

"Don't come near me!" wailed Shimmer Leaf, who then flew to the highest branch of the Changing Tree.

Sky Dance flitted over to Addie's shoulder. "Let me try," she said to Addie, then looked up at Shimmer Leaf. "Shimmer," she cooed. "We went over this earlier. Don't you remember me? I used to come to the caterpillar nursery to sing you songs and read you stories. I'm your big sister!"

"What's a caterpillar?" asked Shimmer

Leaf with a trembling voice. "What's a sister?"

"See what I mean?" said Sky Dance. She sounded like she was about to cry. "We just don't know what to do."

Addie stared long and hard at Shimmer Leaf, filled with sympathy for the butterfly. She wanted so badly to help her, but she'd never seen herself as a saving-the-day kind of girl.

It can't be fun, she thought, *to have no idea who you are, or where you are, or WHY you are.* As she was thinking, her fingers absentmindedly found the bracelet on her wrist. The feel of the smooth, gold chain, and the memory of how wonderful it felt to have a wish come true, sparked an idea.

"Can you tell me more about this 'first

wish' thing?" she asked Sky Dance. "You said she has to find a human child who needs a wish granted. Does she have to find the child herself, or can the child find her?"

Sky Dance thought for a moment. "I don't think it matters. They just have to come together."

A picture was forming in Addie's head, getting clearer by the second. It was a picture of her sister, Clara, as she had watched Addie with Pepper that morning. Clara's face, filled with jealousy, sadness, and loneliness. The face of someone who could really, really use a wish.

"I know what we have to do," said Addie to Sky Dance. "Now it's time to show you *my* home."

🦋 🦋 🦋

As Addie and Sky Dance crossed Silk Meadow, Addie grew anxious about Pepper. She scanned the distance but didn't see him in the spot where she'd left him. If he'd gotten away, she'd have to choose between searching for him and getting Clara to Wishing Wing Grove. It was a choice she didn't want to make.

Suddenly, two little black triangles poked up from the grass. Pepper's ears! Addie laughed with relief.

When she and Sky Dance drew closer, the two butterflies who were standing guard flew to meet them.

"No problems here," said one. "He's kind of sweet and harmless, as dogs go."

"I still don't like them," said the other. "It's that breath. Ugh!"

Addie laughed again, and when Pepper

heard her, he jumped up and started barking.

"Yes, yes. Good boy!" she said as she ran to him and started rubbing his neck. Sky Dance thanked her friends and they headed back toward Wishing Wing Grove.

After she unhooked Pepper's leash from the tree, Addie paused, trying to figure out which way to go from there. She took a step in a certain direction, and it felt right. She took a few more steps, more confident now. "I'm pretty sure this is the way to my house," Addie told Sky Dance as they started walking. "I guess I did know all along."

"Well, actually, you didn't," said Sky Dance with a giggle. "But you do now, because I know." When Addie turned to give her a confused look, Sky Dance flew in a little circle. "Yep. Because I granted you a wish, I'm officially your Wishing Wing. We're connected forever. If we're not too far away from each other, I can send you thoughts and you can send them back!"

"A magic butterfly hotline!" Addie exclaimed.

"Exactly! I can't give you any more wishes, but I can help you in other ways, when you need it."

Something bright and fast in the distance caught Addie's eye. It flitted in and out of the trees. It took Addie a few moments to realize what it was.

A white butterfly.

Addie had always loved these. She'd thought they were just as beautiful as the butterflies who had colors and patterns on their wings, but in a pure and simple way. She felt a tickle on her arm. Sky Dance had landed there to watch the white butterfly too, and Addie was overcome with the worried, nervous thoughts Sky Dance was sending her.

"Oh," said Addie. "That was once a New Bloom, right? It wasn't able to earn its magic and become a Wishing Wing."

Sky Dance nodded sadly. "Mama says that if we can't break the enchantment and the New Blooms lose their magic, all Wishing Wing magic will get weaker. It might even fade forever."

That was too terrible a thought. "I'll do my best to keep that from happening," said Addie. "I promise."

They watched the white butterfly disappear, and then continued walking.

At last, there was the fence of trees, and on the other side of it, the bright yellow wood of Addie's house. Even though it had only been her house for a few days, she was super-glad to see it.

As they crossed into the backyard, Addie told Sky Dance, "Since my mom's home, it's better if Clara comes out here. She won't want to, but I'm an expert at getting her to do things she doesn't want to." She smiled at Sky Dance. "That's part of a big sister's job. You'll find out for yourself soon enough."

Sky Dance landed on the railing of the back deck and said, "I hope so."

Addie put Pepper inside the house, then closed the door and stepped onto the deck again. She found a spot directly underneath Clara's window. It was open, thankfully.

"Clara!" she yelled.

Nothing.

"Hey, Clara!" Addie shouted again.

A few moments passed. Then, a grumpy "What do you want?" came floating down from the open window.

"I have a surprise for you!"

"Nice try. I'm not falling for that trick."

"It's not a trick, cross my heart and pinky promise!"

A pause. "Is it gummy worms?" called Clara.

"Nope. It's better!" replied Addie.

Another pause. "I really don't believe you."

"Look, if you see it and don't think it's

better than gummy worms, I'll give you anything you want from my jewelry box. That's a guarantee."

Now a face appeared in the window, peering down at Addie. Addie hid her hands behind her back and opened her palm. She didn't need to say anything. Sky Dance knew to fly over and land on it.

Clara let out a loud sigh, then her face disappeared. Addie and Sky Dance waited a very long few moments. Was she coming? What would Addie do next if she wasn't coming?

Finally, the back door opened and Clara stepped out, still clutching Squish under one arm.

"I'm here," said Clara. "Show me."

Slowly, Addie brought her hand forward from behind her back. She held up

Sky Dance as if the butterfly were sitting on a pedestal, and resisted the urge to shout "Ta-da!"

Clara's eyes grew wide when she saw Sky Dance, and Addie could see the wonder and delight flickering behind them.

"Is this not the most amazing butterfly you've ever seen?" Addie asked her.

Clara was silent as she stared, stunned, at Sky Dance. Addie kept waiting for her sister to finally smile. But instead, Clara scrunched her face into a frown.

"You always find the good things," she said, pouting.

"Oh, Clara," sighed Addie, and that familiar sisterly tension filled the air between them.

They were quiet for a few moments until a high voice crashed through the silence.

"Hey!" Sky Dance snapped at them. "Not everything is a competition, you know. You're two different people, so it's okay to actually *be* different!"

Clara's jaw dropped open and she took a step back.

"I know," said Addie. "She talks. Also, she has magic. And she needs—*we* need—your help."

Clara shook her head hard. "No way. You *are* tricking me. Stop it!"

Addie whispered to Sky Dance, "Remember how seeing is believing?"

Sky Dance nodded, then took flight, flitting back and forth over the back-yard, searching for something. When she landed, Addie knew she was supposed to bring Clara over. She beckoned to her sister, and fortunately her sister followed.

Sky Dance was sitting on an acorn that was lying in the grass.

"Are you watching, Clara?" asked Addie. Clara shrugged.

Sky Dance fluttered up and flew three circles around the acorn, leaving her personal pink, turquoise, and white rain-bow ribboning behind her. As the colors dissolved into sparkling dust, Clara and Addie both gasped at what had happened.

The acorn was now a tiny seedling with green leaves, just a few inches high.

"Give it ten or fifteen years," said Sky Dance proudly. "That oak tree will be as tall as your house!"

Clara dropped Squish and sank down onto the grass. "Whoa," was all she said.

"Clara," said Addie, kneeling down across from her. "I've discovered something wonderful. And I want to share it with you. Will you let me?"

Maybe it was the word "wonderful," or maybe it was the word "share," but Clara lit up in a way Addie hadn't seen since before their parents had told them they were moving.

"You said something about needing my help?" asked Clara.

Addie and Sky Dance nodded.

"Count me in."

CHAPTER FIVE

O h. My. Gosh." That was all Clara could say as she stood at the entrance to Wishing Wing Grove. Addie laughed. She couldn't remember the last time she'd seen her sister at a loss for words.

"I know," Addie told her. "We can take a tour later, but right now we need to go straight to the Changing Tree."

On their way from the house, Addie and Sky Dance had told Clara all about Wishing Wings and New Blooms. She'd learned about their magic, the mysterious dark enchantment, and, of course, Shimmer Leaf. Now, as they followed Sky Dance through the grove, Clara kept stumbling, too busy looking around in amazement to watch her step. She'd brought along her purple satin backpack, filled with juice boxes, graham crackers, and, of course, Squish.

"Ever since we moved in, I've been watching the woods out my window," whispered Clara, as she stared at a beautiful black, white, and silver Wishing Wing soaring past them. "I had a feeling there was something special out here, but who knew it would be *magically* special!"

She doesn't know the half of it, thought Addie, but she wasn't ready to tell Clara about how she'd been turned into a butterfly. She liked keeping that to herself, at least for a little while.

As they neared the Changing Tree, Sky Dance flitted close to Addie and asked, "What should we do once we get them together?"

"I'm not sure," Addie said. "I haven't thought that far yet."

"Remember, even though it doesn't matter how they meet, Clara still has to catch Shimmer Leaf, then set her free. It's pretty simple when a New Bloom knows what she's supposed to do, but Shimmer won't be caught so easily."

Addie nodded, hoping that between

her, Clara, and Sky Dance, they'd come up with a plan.

The afternoon sun was lower when they finally arrived, and the slanted light made the Changing Tree glow like a lantern in the shade of the grove.

"Wow," said Clara, putting her hand on the thick bark of the trunk and peering into the hollow to see the three gray chrysalides. "This is really happening."

"Shimmer Leaf's up here," called Sky Dance as she flew into the branches.

Addie pointed to show Clara, but then dropped her arm, suddenly confused.

Shimmer Leaf wasn't there.

Sky Dance fluttered frantically in and out of the other branches, higher and higher, finally squeaking "She's gone!" from the top of the tree.

Gone? Addie hadn't even thought of that possibility. Shimmer Leaf had seemed too afraid to move.

"I saw it all!" cried an excited voice. Addie looked down. At her feet sat something green and red. Madame Furia. Addie lowered her hand and let the caterpillar climb on, then brought her close to her face. Clara came to listen and Sky Dance landed on Addie's arm.

"What did you see?" Addie asked Madame Furia.

"Oh, it was awful," she said, her eyes rolling around in tiny circles. "I was on my way back home when I saw two gigantic blue wasps surround Shimmer Leaf on that branch. They were buzzing so loudly, it hurt my ears! Every time she flew to a new branch, they followed her. She hopped higher and higher and those wasps kept buzzing louder and louder! Finally, she had no choice but to fly away from the  tree. The wasps chased her . . . and that was the last I saw of any of them." Madame Furia's entire body trembled, segment by segment. "The poor thing! And your mother and father are going to be so worried!"

"We'll find her," said Sky Dance. "We have *two* human girls helping us now."

Madame Furia's red eyes looked Clara up and down. "So I see," she said. "Thank goodness!"

"Please go tell my parents what's

happening!" Sky Dance urged Madame Furia. "Tell them to send every Wishing Wing to search the woods. We'll find her, and everything's going to be okay."

Addie put Madame Furia back on the ground, and they watched her inch away as fast as she could.

"Do you really believe that?" Addie asked Sky Dance. "That everything will be okay?"

Sky Dance slowly flapped her wings twice, and Addie realized that must be the butterfly version of a shrug.

"What choice do I have?" replied Sky Dance. "You can't have courage without confidence."

As soon as Sky Dance said it, Addie felt that confidence fill her. This thought-connection really came in handy!

"I think we should split up and search in different directions," said Clara as she sipped on a juice box.

"That makes sense," said Sky Dance. "I can cover a lot more ground flying than you can. Clara, you should stay in the grove, because when we do find Shimmer Leaf, we'll need to know where you are. We have to get you together quickly. Addie, can you take Clara and search around here? I'll fly out into the woods and help the other Wishing Wings."

"Where do wasps usually hang out in the grove?" asked Addie. "Maybe we can start there."

"That's the strangest part," replied Sky Dance. "I've never seen wasps in the grove. They have their own realm nearby, but they know they're not welcome here.

Coming in and causing trouble would break the Great Wasp–Butterfly Peace Treaty created by my grandmother and the old Wasp Queen. That queen died a little while ago. They have a new one now."

Hmmm, thought Addie. Maybe the wasps were not a random coincidence, but rather, part of some bigger problem. Well, they didn't have time to figure it out. The only thing that mattered right then was finding Shimmer Leaf. The sun was sinking lower every minute.

A cluster of other Wishing Wings zoomed through the air above, and Sky Dance rose up to join them. Addie and Clara waved goodbye as they watched the patchwork of brilliant, fluttering colors disappear into the distance. Addie sent her strongest *Good luck!* thoughts to her butterfly friend.

"So," said Clara as she stuffed her empty juice box into her backpack, then grabbed Squish and tucked him under one arm. "Where do we look first?"

Addie led Clara as they backtracked through Addie's flight as a butterfly, starting with the caterpillar nursery, then the creek, then the stretch of boulders where she'd first met Sky Dance's royal parents. Clara kept pausing to touch every surface she could—moss, grass, water, bark, leaves, rock—and let out a bewildered "Ooooh" each time.

Again and again the sisters called, "Shimmer Leaf!" pausing to listen for buzzing wasps or a high, trembling voice. They stood at the base of every tree and peered up, scanning the branches and leaves for flashes of Shimmer Leaf's purple, peach, and mint-green wings. Addie and Clara climbed onto each large rock to get just a little closer to the sky, watching for the smallest movement anywhere.

"This is pointless," said Addie after a while, collapsing onto a rock. "We're

stuck here on the ground. How can we find a butterfly who may have flown far away and could be fifty feet high in a tree?"

"It would be worse if we were just sitting around, doing nothing," said Clara as she hopped from one boulder to the next.

"I guess you're right," agreed Addie.

Clara paused and spun around. "Wait! You're saying I'm right?"

"Oh, be quiet. It's not the first time I've ever said you were right."

"It sure feels like it," Clara huffed.

Addie stood up to move away from her sister. She was annoyed now. Why couldn't they get along, even in an enchanted grove? As she took a step onto the next rock, she heard a noise. It was faint, and strange, and very sad.

"Clara, did you hear that?" whispered Addie.

She pointed down. Clara made her way to Addie's rock and they listened again. Clara's face lit up.

"I did! It sounded like something crying."

"It sounded like *Shimmer Leaf* crying!" exclaimed Addie, and without thinking, she held up her hand to Clara. Clara slapped her high-five, and they both shouted, "YES!"

Then another, very different noise rose up from the calm. This noise was angry and threatening. It grew louder and louder. Both girls turned in the direction it was coming from.

Two blazingly blue wasps—each one twice as big as any wasp Addie had ever seen—were flying straight toward them at top speed.

CHAPTER SIX

D uck!" yelled Addie. She jumped down behind the boulder, pulling Clara with her.

The wasps raced past like fighter jets, making almost as much noise. Addie could hear one of them laugh wickedly as it went over their heads.

Why did it have to be wasps? When Addie was five, she'd stepped on a small one and it stung her foot. She still remembered how much that hurt and couldn't imagine what a sting from these much bigger bugs would feel like.

"Are they gone?" asked Clara after the buzzing faded, but as soon as she did, the buzzing grew louder again. Both girls stuck their heads up. The wasps were circling back! The girls crouched down again, and Addie grabbed a nearby stick to fight them off. But the wasps didn't attack. They landed on a rock, both of them laughing hard.

"That was great!" shouted one, who sounded female. "We haven't had the chance to scare a human kid in a long time!"

"Look at them down there," said the other. This one sounded like a boy. "They're curled up like little snails! They won't get in our way."

"Hey, humans!" taunted the first wasp. "Thanks for helping us find the New Bloom!"

Addie winced. It had never occurred to her that the wasps might be watching them search for Shimmer Leaf.

"So, Poke," said the boy wasp. "What next?"

Addie could see the wasps through a gap between two rocks. She watched the girl wasp fly down to the spot where they'd heard Shimmer Leaf's sobs.

"You were right, Striker. She's definitely in some kind of crevice, where these two rocks come together," Poke said. "But it's a really small opening. We can't squeeze in there to get her."

"Ha!" laughed Striker. "I never thought being big would be a problem!" He flew down to land next to Poke. "Can't we just keep her here until sunset, when her magic disappears?"

"Don't be dumb," sneered Poke. "We have specific orders to chase her back to the Wasp Realm."

Addie and Clara looked at each other with alarm.

"We can't let that happen," whispered Clara.

"But if we run to get help, they'll come after us . . ." Addie whispered back, but then she realized something important. "Wait a minute! I don't have to *run*! I can *think*!"

Addie had forgotten to send Sky Dance a message that they'd found Shimmer Leaf. She knew she just had to think the words WE FOUND HER! PLEASE HELP US! COME QUICK! as hard as she could, and Sky Dance would hear her.

"If only we could distract the wasps," said Addie.

"Or maybe we could trick them somehow," added Clara.

Clara's suggestion set off an idea in Addie's head. For a minute or so, everything was eerily quiet and tense as the wasps paced in front of the crevice and

Addie focused on her idea. Then she heard a *flit-flut* near her ear and turned to see Sky Dance sitting on her shoulder.

Addie opened her mouth to say something, but Sky Dance whispered, "Shhh! We don't want them to know she's here."

"Who?" asked Addie softly.

"My mom. The queen." Sky Dance pointed an antenna at Addie's knee, where Queen Rose Glow was now landing, looking very sad.

"Oh," sighed Queen Rose Glow. "I can hear Shimmer Leaf crying. My poor baby!"

"I think I have a plan," said Addie. She then leaned close to Sky Dance's antennae to tell her. When she was done, Sky Dance's eyes lit up.

"Is that even possible?" asked Addie.

"I think so!" replied Sky Dance. She

flew over to her mother and murmured to her. The queen looked at Addie, then nodded excitedly.

Addie turned to Clara. "Something's going to happen. Don't freak out."

Before Clara could say a word, Sky Dance and Rose Glow took flight, touching their wings together to spout the rainbow of their combined colors. As they circled Addie three times, strands of pink, turquoise, white, red, green, and silver filled the air with sparkles.

Clara watched, her jaw hanging open.

When all the glitter faded before Addie's eyes, she didn't bother to examine herself. She knew there was no time for that. Instead, she flapped her newly formed butterfly wings and took off as fast as she could. The ground fell away below her, and the air rushing past felt natural and familiar. It was like she'd always been flying!

She knew that to the stunned Clara, it looked like her sister was gone and in her place was a Wishing Wing butterfly.

She also knew that to the wasps, she looked like Shimmer Leaf. Sky Dance and Rose Glow had used their magic to turn Addie's butterfly wings the same colors as Shimmer Leaf's. The leaf patterns were not there—she understood that patterns were special to each Wishing Wing and couldn't be copied—but she hoped the wasps wouldn't notice.

"Poke!" Addie heard Striker yell. "She's making a break for it!"

"Let's get her!" shouted Poke. "Nice try, butterfly! We're too fast for you!"

Addie felt Sky Dance sending her a thought message. *Head for the two tall pine trees to the south*, it said. *Fly until you turn human again, and we'll take care of the rest.*

As she flew toward the pine trees, Addie could hear the wasps buzzing behind her, but her head start kept them at a distance. This was just like the time she raced a girl named Jillian in gym class at her old school. Jillian usually beat her at everything, but on that day, Addie had sprinted from the word "Go!" and didn't look back until she crossed the finish line first. Addie remembered how proud she'd been to realize she was a faster runner than she'd thought, and that powered her butterfly wings now.

Addie kept flapping as hard as she could and found a breeze, which gave her an extra push. The pine trees were getting closer and closer . . . while the wasps' buzzing grew louder and louder . . .

She'd made it! Addie flew right through the space between the two pine trees.

Then, with a *thump*, she fell backward on the ground. In an instant, she had all of her usual parts and was Addie-size again.

The wasps sped by. The branches of the pine trees had blocked their view and they hadn't seen Addie change into a human. She caught her breath and watched as two bright Wishing Wings, then four, then ten, flew into the gap between the trees. Still more butter-flies came, flying so close to one another she couldn't tell where one butterfly's wings ended and another's began. The flickering colors looked like a giant kaleidoscope.

They were filling the gap between the pine trees. *A net!* Addie realized.

Suddenly, Queen Rose Glow flew up to her.

"Are you all right, my dear?" she asked.

"Yes, I'm fine!"

"Run back to Sky Dance and your sis-ter! We'll hold the wasps back with some group magic."

Addie nodded, jumped up, dusted her-self off, and raced back to the rocks.

When she got there, she found Clara kneeling on the ground in front of

Shimmer Leaf's hiding place. Sky Dance perched on a rock nearby, staring nervously in the direction of the sun. The bottom tip of it had dropped behind the treetops, and the sky was tinted pink. It wouldn't be long before it was completely gone.

Clara put her face as close as she could to the crevice's opening. Addie could still hear Shimmer Leaf's sobs coming from inside.

"Shimmer Leaf," Clara said softly to the butterfly. "I understand that you're scared. I understand that you're lonely. I know exactly how that feels, because I just found myself in a brand-new place, too."

Clara paused, and they listened. It was quiet. The sobs had stopped.

"But now I see that I'm not alone at all," continued Clara. "There are friends around me everywhere. Some, I just haven't met yet."

Clara glanced quickly at Addie. Addie smiled back.

Clara took a deep breath and put her face to the crevice once more. "Can I be your first new friend, Shimmer Leaf?"

A tiny, shaking voice said, "Okay."

"Here," said Clara, reaching as much of her hand into the opening as would fit. "Climb on. I'll help you out of there."

Addie held her breath, and she knew Sky Dance was doing the same. They waited for a long moment. Addie glanced up to see that even more of the sun had disappeared, and her heart thudded harder.

Clara pulled her hand out of the crevice and clapped the other one on top. She smiled big. Shimmer Leaf must be inside!

"I've got you," whispered Clara to her hands. "You're safe with me."

"Are you sure?" asked the tiny voice.

Clara opened her palms.

A burst of color shot into the air and fluttered away.

CHAPTER SEVEN

N o!" shouted Clara as they watched
Shimmer Leaf dart toward the sky.
"Where is she going?"

Sky Dance began chasing her sister,
but then paused in midair. Shimmer Leaf
was slowing down. She flew in a U-shape
and headed back toward them, landing
gently on Clara's still-open palm.

"Clara!" said Shimmer Leaf. Her voice didn't sound scared anymore. It rang out bright and happy. "You caught me, then set me free! That means I'm your Wishing Wing!"

Sky Dance rushed to land next to Shimmer Leaf.

"Shimmer Leaf!" she cried. "Do you know who you are?"

Shimmer Leaf touched her wing to Sky Dance's. "Yes, Sky, of course. Why wouldn't I?" She let out a huff and turned back to Clara. "Sisters can be so irritating."

Sky Dance laughed and said, "The enchantment's broken!" She flew two joyful flips in the air.

"Yay!" cheered Addie. "Nice work, Clara!" Then she caught sight of the sun and remembered there was one more, very important thing they still had to do. "Shimmer Leaf! The wish!"

"Oh!" exclaimed Shimmer Leaf, looking at the pink-and-red-striped sky. "Where did the day go?" She turned to Clara. "I'm here to make a wish come true for you."

"Really? That's amazing!" said Clara, pretending she didn't already know it. She winked at Addie and Sky Dance. She'd had a little time to think about her wish, but made a face like she was just deciding now. "You know what I've always wished for? A pet of my very own."

"A pet of your very own . . ." echoed Shimmer Leaf, nodding. "That's a great wish. Let's see, I think I can make that happen."

She looked around, her antennae pointing back and forth. Squish was lying on a nearby rock. Clara must have left him there when she went to coax Shimmer Leaf out of her hiding spot. When Shimmer Leaf spotted him, she shot into the air. In an instant, she was wrapping Squish in her glittering purple, peach, and mint-green rainbow. After her third time around, she landed.

They all watched the sparkles shimmer and blink. Addie couldn't wait to see what would appear in Squish's place! She laced her fingers through Clara's and squeezed her sister's hand.

But when the colors and sparkles vanished, there was nothing there.

No Squish. No real live pet.

"What happened?" Clara burst out, nearly in tears. "Where's Squish?"

Sky Dance and Shimmer Leaf didn't answer. They were both looking at the last tiny bit of sun as it fell behind the treetops. It was officially sunset. Sky Dance turned to her sister and looked her up and down.

"You're still a Wishing Wing!" she remarked. "We did it!"

"You mean, I earned my magic?" asked Shimmer Leaf.

"Yes! Yes! Thanks to Addie and Clara! I'll tell you the whole story later. I have a feeling these girls have to get home right away."

"Where's Squish?" cried Clara.

"That's why you have to get home," replied Shimmer Leaf with a mischievous smile. "Hurry! There's someone there who needs you."

Clara gasped excitedly and grabbed her backpack. "Come on!" she said to Addie.

Addie led her sister a few steps in the direction of Silk Meadow, then suddenly stopped. She turned back to the butterflies.

"When will we see you again?" called Addie.

"If the next chrysalis opens and we have the same problem . . . then very soon, I'm sure," answered Sky Dance. "Maybe even tomorrow! We'll need your help finding children who need wishes."

"We'll be ready!"

"We will?" whispered Clara to her. "We don't know any other kids here."

"We don't know them *yet*," said Addie. "But you said yourself: there are friends everywhere."

Clara grinned. "I did say that, didn't I?" She waved to their first two new friends. "Goodbye, Sky Dance! Goodbye, Shimmer Leaf!"

The butterfly sisters flitted into the air, flapping their wings in their own special kind of wave.

"Let's go!" said Addie. She grabbed Clara's hand again and they raced toward home.

🦋 🦋 🦋

They ran until they reached the border between the woods and their house, then stopped to catch their breath.

"Hey, Addie," said Clara, watching a

bird fly overhead. "That turning-into-a-butterfly thing was pretty crazy. But did you notice how I didn't freak out?"

"Yes, I'm so glad," Addie replied.

"However," said Clara with a serious face now. "I will if I don't get a turn to do that, too!"

Addie couldn't help but laugh. "I understand. Hopefully, there will be a chance next time."

They stepped through the trees that bordered their backyard. It felt strange, yet wonderful, to be back where their adventure had started just a short time ago.

Clara began looking frantically around. "Shimmer Leaf said there was something here that needed us . . ." she said. "But I don't see anything. Do you?"

Addie walked a circle around the yard, but didn't notice anything either.

"She could have given us a hint," said Clara, frustrated. She picked up a log from the woodpile to peek underneath.

"Maybe she didn't think we needed it," said Addie. She thought for a moment, then remembered something. "Hey," she added. "When we were searching for Shimmer Leaf, we found her by listening. Maybe we should do that now."

They were quiet for a few moments. Addie heard the wind whistle through the trees, the neighbors laughing next door, and a car rumbling down the road.

Then, she heard something else:

Mew.

"Addie!" Clara exclaimed.

"I heard it, too!"

"Where is it coming from?"

Mew. Mew, mew.

"I think it's coming from under the deck!" said Addie. They both rushed to the side of the deck, where there was a small space between the wooden boards and the ground. Addie was about to crawl under, but then stopped herself.

This was Clara's wish. It was Clara's discovery, and Clara's moment. She didn't want to take that from her sister.

Addie stepped aside and motioned for Clara to go ahead.

Clara dropped to her knees and disappeared under the deck. A few moments later, she reappeared, scrambling backward with one hand.

In the other, she clutched a tiny, orange-striped kitten. He had big blue eyes just like Squish, and smudges of dirt on his face and paws just like him, too.

Mew, the kitten cried, but he sounded less frightened and lonely now.

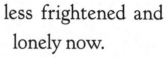

Clara stood up and hugged the kitten, kissing his fuzzy little head.

"Squish!" she cooed softly to him.

Addie had never seen her sister so filled with joy. It was like she'd never been sad, or angry, or lonely in her life.

The back door slid open, and Addie's mother and father stepped out.

"Addie, there you are!" exclaimed

Mom. "Have you girls been outside this whole time?"

"Yup," said Addie. It wasn't a lie, after all.

"What's that you've got there?" asked Dad when he noticed the fluff of orange nuzzled under Clara's chin.

"We found a kitten under the deck!" said Clara. "Isn't he the cutest, sweetest thing ever?"

"He looks just like your Squish," remarked Dad.

"He must belong to someone," said Mom.

He belongs to Clara, thought Addie, but she knew she couldn't say that. Instead, she said: "Can we take care of him until we find the owner? If there isn't an owner, can we keep him?"

Mom and Dad looked at Clara. There was no denying it: Clara had never seemed happier. Addie's parents exchanged a long glance, then finally smiled.

"Okay," said Mom. "Let's bring him in and clean him up. The poor thing must be hungry!"

Mom and Dad went inside, and Clara followed. As she passed Addie, Addie could hear Squish—a real live breathing Squish!—purr like a loud motorboat engine. Addie knew that if humans could purr, Clara would be doing it, too.

Before Addie went into the house, she turned to stare at the woods. Now she knew so much about them: There were dangers and dark enchantments out there, but also wonders beyond her imagination. Every New Bloom who needed their help earning its magic would mean another set of challenges.

Addie felt a flutter in her stomach.

She couldn't wait for the next adventure to begin.

Butterfly Wishes

Tiger Streak's Tale

PROLOGUE

An early morning breeze whistled through the woods, making the leaves of a huge willow tree shimmy and shake. Two butterflies sat perched on the edge of a deep hollow in the tree's trunk, and the breeze made their colorful wings ripple.

The butterflies barely noticed. They were busy staring into the hollow, where they saw three small gray shapes hanging down. Each one was a chrysalis, and inside were caterpillars waiting to emerge as something beautiful and new.

One of the butterflies, Sky Dance, had pink and turquoise wings splattered with cloud patterns. She pointed one of her antennae to a fourth shape: the crumpled remains of a chrysalis that had already opened.

"Just yesterday, you were right in there," she whispered to the other butterfly, Shimmer Leaf.

"Whoa," muttered Shimmer Leaf, stretching her wings out flat. They were bright purple, peach, and mint green with leaf patterns. "Wishing Wing chrysalides should be glowing and gold . . . but these just look wrong."

"We suspect there's a dark enchantment on them," said Sky Dance. "When you emerged, you didn't know who you were, or even that you were a Wishing Wing!"

"I was so scared . . ." said Shimmer Leaf, shuddering at the memory.

"The worst part was that you didn't know you had to earn your magic by granting a wish to a human child before sunset. You almost lost your magic forever, and all Wishing Wing magic would have been weakened!" Sky Dance paused, staring sadly into the hollow. "I'm worried that these chrysalides will have the same problem."

"Who would cast a dark enchantment like this?" asked Shimmer Leaf. "Who would want to make Wishing Wing magic disappear?"

"We don't know, but hopefully we'll find out soon."

Suddenly, one of the gray chrysalides began to move, wiggling and jiggling. It wasn't because of the breeze.

This chrysalis was getting ready to burst.

"I'm nervous," Shimmer Leaf said softly, touching one of her wings to one of Sky Dance's wings.

"Me too," replied Sky Dance. "But we have to be strong and brave. If our friend is under enchantment, she'll need our help."

"And we'll have to find it on the far side of the meadow," added Shimmer Leaf.

The sisters exchanged a glance. They both knew what that meant.

They turned back to the chrysalis just as it began to open . . .

CHAPTER ONE

Addie Gibson opened her eyes.
A stream of golden morning sunlight peeked past her window curtains. She sat up in bed and looked around. For a moment, everything felt the same as it had the day before.

Her room was still filled with unpacked boxes, since her family had just moved to a new house. The walls were bare with that half-gross, half-sweet smell of fresh turquoise paint. Her best friend, Violet, was still far away, back in the city where Addie used to live, and her new neighborhood, Brook Forest, was still surrounded by way too much nature.

Then she remembered:

Butterflies! Wishes!

MAGIC!

Yesterday had been the day Addie discovered it all.

Deep in the woods behind her house, there was a secret grove filled with enchanted butterflies called Wishing Wings. They could talk, grant wishes, and work extraordinary magic. The Wishing Wings needed Addie and her younger sister, Clara, to help newly hatched butterflies earn their magic by making a wish come true for a human child. Someone, or some*thing*, had cast a dark enchantment on these "New Blooms." If Addie and Clara didn't succeed in their task, the New Blooms would lose their powers forever and weaken the magic of all the Wishing Wings.

Addie shuddered at the thought as she touched the gold bracelet on her wrist. It kept her close to Violet—that had been the wish her new friend, the Wishing Wing princess Sky Dance, granted her. Sky Dance believed another New Bloom would emerge today who might need help granting its first wish. Addie and Sky Dance could share thoughts if they were near each other, so Addie listened hard inside her head.

But she heard only silence, until . . .

"Stop! Stop it now!"

It was Clara shouting from across the

hallway. Addie burst out of bed and into Clara's room.

Clara was huddled in a corner, cradling a little ball of orange fur to her chest: her new kitten, Squish. Clara had helped Shimmer Leaf, Sky Dance's sister and the first of the newly hatched Wishing Wings, break her enchantment by catching the butterfly and then setting her free. In return, Shimmer Leaf granted Clara's wish for a real live pet of her own . . . and now Clara's stuffed kitten was a real one.

The magic of it had been amazing, but not as amazing as seeing Clara snap out of her sadness about moving to Brook Forest.

Even Addie's parents were happy about Squish joining the family—they thought he was a stray kitten the girls found in the backyard. Only Addie's dog, Pepper, wasn't a fan of their new feline friend. Right now he was running back and forth in front of Clara, barking at Squish.

"Pepper!" snapped Addie, grabbing his collar. "Bad boy!"

She picked him up and put him out of the room, then closed the door.

"I'm sorry, Clara," she said, kneeling on the floor next to her sister. "Sorry to you, too, Squish. Pepper has to get used to the fact that he's no longer the only cute one in the house!"

Addie reached out to pet Squish. He instantly started purring and stretched out on the floor. She rubbed his soft orange-and-white-striped belly.

"Can you believe it?" asked Clara. "I woke up and thought maybe it was all just a dream, but then I felt this fuzzy warm thing curled up next to me."

"I know," said Addie. "It seems unreal to me, too. But it *was* real, wasn't it?"

Clara nodded, smiling, then stood up and went to her window. It looked out on their backyard and the woods beyond. Addie joined her.

"What do you think Sky Dance and Shimmer Leaf are doing right now?" asked Clara. "When do you think we'll see them again?"

"I don't know," replied Addie. "But I have a feeling it'll be soon."

Clara slid open her window and rested her forehead against the screen, breathing in the fresh morning air. "I think I could get used to living in the country."

Suddenly, voices came drifting through the open window. They were kid voices, but not happy ones. Someone was yelling at someone else. They sounded pretty mad.

Clara shot Addie a curious look.

"I'll go investigate," said Addie.

"You mean, *eavesdrop*?" teased Clara.

"Hey, stop picking up big words from Mom and Dad. I can be curious, can't I?"

Addie got dressed with lightning speed. She rushed downstairs and out the back door.

"I can't believe you!" shouted a boy's voice. "You ruined it!"

"I didn't mean to!" came a girl's voice, just as loud and angry.

Addie heard a loud *thump*. She watched as a soccer ball came crashing through the bushes that separated her yard from the one next door.

"That's what I think of your art project!" yelled the boy.

The ball rolled to a stop right in front of the deck. Addie picked it up and stood there for a few moments. She looked up at Clara's window, where Clara had been watching with Squish in her arms. Clara shrugged, then disappeared.

"Hi," came a voice.

Addie turned to see a girl standing at the bushes. She seemed about the same age as Addie, with long red hair in a braid. She wore a T-shirt with the collar cut off, and two different kinds of sneakers. *Well,* thought Addie, *at least her socks match.*

"Hi," Addie said, and held up the ball. "Is this yours?"

Now Addie could see that the ball had been painted all white, with a goofy face on it. The face had wide eyes, a big nose, and a crooked smile. It even had earrings and a patch of curly red hair.

Addie couldn't help it—she let out a
laugh.

"This is a really good face!" she said.

"Thanks," said the girl, but she looked
embarrassed about it.

"I'm Addie. We just moved in a few
days ago."

"I'm Morgan."

They were quiet as Morgan approached
and took the ball. It was awkward, meeting new people. Even ones who live right
next door.

The bushes rustled, and now a woman
appeared on the edge of the yard.

"Hey, Mom," called Morgan when she saw the woman. "This is Addie, our new neighbor. Addie, this is my mom."

Morgan's mom smiled and waved. "Otherwise known as Mrs. Werner. I was planning to bring over some cookies tomorrow, so we could all meet properly. But I see that, once again, Morgan has gone and done things her own way."

She gave Morgan a stern look.

"Calvin kicked the ball over here!" said Morgan. "I was just getting it back."

"Oh," said Mrs. Werner, but her expression grew even more stern. "Yes, he told me you destroyed his new soccer ball."

"I thought it was an old one he doesn't use anymore!" Morgan added.

Mrs. Werner shook her head. "Honey, you can't keep painting things that aren't supposed to be painted. I bought you paper and blank canvases. Paint those!"

"But . . ." protested Morgan.

"Addie, it was nice meeting you," said Mrs. Werner. "Tell your parents I'm looking forward to meeting them too."

Mrs. Werner went back to her yard.

Morgan sighed. She looked at the ball again and then at Addie. "But I don't want to paint on paper or canvas," she said softly. "I just like taking real things and making them look different. Mom doesn't understand. She calls me The Troublemaker."

Addie smiled back. "That's a good one. My mom calls me Little Miss Overthink."

Morgan and Addie laughed together. The awkwardness was gone, and Addie felt more comfortable now. *Hey!* she thought. *We might like each other!*

Would Morgan be her first new friend in Brook Forest? *Human* friend, that is?

A moment later, Addie heard and felt something flutter past her ear. She looked up to see a flash of color in the air above.

Make that two flashes of color.

It was Sky Dance and Shimmer Leaf!

As soon as Addie realized this, she felt Sky Dance's thoughts in her head. *Quick! Get Clara! Meet us in the woods!*

This could mean only one thing: another New Bloom had emerged, and the Wishing Wings needed help!

"I'm so sorry," said Addie to Morgan as she started backing away. "There's kind of an emergency. I've got to find my sister right now."

Morgan looked confused. "An emergency?"

"I can't explain it. I just have to go."

Now Morgan looked deeply hurt. She dropped her head and turned toward the bushes, her shoulders sagging.

Addie watched Morgan walk away, imagining Morgan's point of view. To her, it must have looked like Addie had suddenly, randomly, changed her mind about talking to Morgan. But that was totally not the case!

Addie wasn't sure what else to say, so she didn't say anything.

She just ran into the house, feeling absolutely awful. She vowed to herself to make it up to Morgan somehow. But right now, Sky Dance and Shimmer Leaf were depending on her.

CHAPTER TWO

C lara!" shouted Addie to her sister's window. "Come quick! The butterflies need us!"

But Clara was already stepping out the back door. Addie jumped, startled.

"I know," said Clara. "I got the same message from Shimmer."

"We should tell Mom that we're going for a walk."

"Already done."

Addie was impressed. "Nice work."

"I think of things, too, you know," said Clara, but she didn't sound mad. Just proud of herself.

Addie reached out and took her sister's hand. Together, they walked past the row of evenly spaced trees at the back edge of their yard and into the thick, green world of the woods.

Addie was surprised to find she already recognized certain trees and rocks. It really was becoming *their* woods now, after just a day! She couldn't help but smile, remembering how scared she'd been of all this twenty-four hours ago.

Eventually, the girls reached Silk Meadow, a sun-drenched clearing of tall grass that marked the entrance to

Wishing Wing Grove. Addie felt something land on her arm. A familiar tickle.

"Hi, Sky Dance," she said, raising her arm so she was eye level with her butterfly friend. "Long time no see."

Sky Dance flapped her wings. They were just as big and beautiful as Addie remembered. Sky Dance tilted her furry pink head as if she were thinking hard. Her big, dark eyes, which were as smooth and shiny as beads, gazed into Addie's.

"You know what's strange?" Sky Dance asked Addie in her high, clear voice. "I woke up this morning and had to remind myself that yesterday really happened!"

"Same here!" exclaimed Addie, and they both laughed.

Addie saw Clara holding out her palm for Shimmer Leaf to land on.

"Hello again," said Clara to Shimmer Leaf. "How was your first night as a butterfly?"

Shimmer Leaf stretched out her new wings. They were bright purple, peach, and mint green with leaf patterns. "Once I figured out how to tuck these things in for sleeping," she said, "it was great!"

The two girls and the two butterflies all giggled again, then fell silent . . . and serious.

"You called us," said Addie. "Does that mean . . ."

"Yes," replied Sky Dance. "Another New Bloom came out of her chrysalis this morning."

"It's our cousin Tiger Streak," added Shimmer Leaf.

"Was it just like with Shimmer?" asked Addie. Shimmer Leaf had woken up not knowing who she was, or that she had to grant a wish before sunset. It had taken

lots of quick thinking, plus a dash of courage, for Clara to catch the butterfly and set her free.

"We're not sure," said Sky Dance. "She flew away from the Changing Tree before we could talk to her. But she's been seen throughout the grove."

"You mean *heard* throughout the grove," corrected Shimmer Leaf.

Sky Dance sighed. "That too."

"What do you mean?" asked Clara.

"Apparently," said Sky Dance, "Tiger Streak is fluttering around making a very *un*-butterfly-like noise."

"*Bzzz*," added Shimmer Leaf.

"Like a bee?" asked Addie, frowning.

"Exactly," said Sky Dance.

"That, uh, seems like a bad sign," said Clara.

"*Exactly*," agreed Shimmer Leaf. "Will

you help us find her? We'll also need to find a human child to catch her and set her free to break the enchantment. Then Tiger Streak can grant that child a wish and earn her magic."

"We'll do whatever we can," Clara said.

"We're ready," Addie assured them.

The butterflies took flight again, and the girls followed them across the meadow. As they stepped through the entrance of Wishing Wing Grove, Sky Dance led them toward a large boulder. At first glance, it looked like someone had covered it with a thousand rainbow sprinkles. But Addie knew the boulder was crowded with dozens of Wishing Wing butterflies gathered together, each one with a dazzling combination of colors and patterns on its wings. She'd never seen anything so beautiful . . . and couldn't imagine who, or what, would want to drain these creatures of their magic.

At the top of the boulder sat Sky Dance and Shimmer Leaf's parents, Queen Rose Glow and King Flit Flash.

"Addie, Clara, my dears!" said Rose Glow. "Welcome back!"

Rose Glow's name suddenly made sense to Addie: her red, green, and silver wings sparkled in the sunlight, making the rose patterns on them light up.

"Thank you," said Addie and Clara at the same time. Sky Dance landed on Addie's shoulder, and Shimmer Leaf landed on Clara's.

"No, thank *you*," said Flit Flash. "We have our Shimmer Leaf back, and we'll be forever grateful." His wings were blue and black, with white lightning bolts on

them. They reminded Addie of a toy race car she once had.

"We did get lucky," said Addie. "Our plan worked just in the nick of time."

"Don't be so modest," chirped a cheerful voice from the boulder. "I think you had more than luck on your side."

Addie saw Madame Furia sitting next to the queen. She was the queen's green caterpillar friend, and her story was a sad one: when she was young, she'd broken a rule, and as punishment was never allowed to change into a Wishing Wing. It didn't seem to get her down, though.

"You had smarts, and you used them," continued Madame Furia. "Feel proud of that! It's another kind of magic. I know I use it." She winked at Addie, and one of her long antennae dipped forward as if she were raising an eyebrow.

BZZZ!

Something yellow, orange, and black suddenly streaked past overhead.

"That's her!" shouted Shimmer Leaf.

Another something streaked past, right behind Tiger Streak. This something was yellow and black. It also made a *bzzz* noise, but a much more natural-sounding one.

"With a bee?" asked Sky Dance.

"That bee's been chasing Tiger Streak all morning!" said the queen.

"Let's go!" Addie said, taking off after the two zigzagging insects. She could hear Clara's footsteps right behind her.

Sky Dance and Shimmer Leaf flew

straight as arrows up ahead, their wings beating fast.

Then, Addie heard a loud *thump*.

"Ow!" yelled Clara.

Addie skidded to a stop and saw Clara twenty feet behind her, facedown in a berry bramble. She ran to help her sister, grabbing her hand and pulling her up. Clara's arms and legs were covered in scratches. Tears pooled in her eyes, and she bit her lip hard. Addie knew that meant Clara was trying her best not to cry.

"Are you okay?" asked Addie, brushing some berries off her sister's shirt.

Clara just bit her lip harder and nodded.

Sky Dance and Shimmer Leaf circled back. Flit Flash and Rose Glow must have seen Clara fall, too, and flew quickly toward them. The Wishing Wing royal family landed, one by one, on a berry bush.

"We don't want anyone getting hurt," said Rose Glow. "What would you say to a quick little flight with Sky and Shimmer?"

Clara's face lit up. She knew exactly what that meant. "I would say, yes please!"

Addie laughed. "I knew you'd get your chance!"

Yesterday, the Wishing Wings had turned Addie into a butterfly for a short time. Needless to say, it had been spectacular. Clara was desperately hoping for a turn.

By now, all the butterflies from the boulder had flown over to see what was happening. They were eager to watch some very special magic that only the Wishing Wing royal family could create.

Rose Glow and Sky Dance began flying around Clara, close to each other with their wings touching, while Flit Flash and Shimmer Leaf did the same with Addie. Each pair of butterflies left a shimmering ribbon of their combined colors in their wake. Each pair flew three times around the girls.

Addie closed her eyes and could still see the colors popping behind her eyelids. When they stopped, she opened them. Everything looked different because she was smaller. Butterfly-size. She turned her head to see her wings. They were the same ones as last time: magenta and powder blue, with heart patterns.

Next to her, there was another butterfly. Her wings were deep pink and orange, like a sunset, and patterned with flames.

Ha! thought Addie. *That's my sister, all right. She's full of fire.*

"Whoa!" shouted Clara, examining her butterfly-self.

When Addie had first been turned into a butterfly, it took her a few moments to get the hang of it—she had to really think about what it would feel like to fly. But Clara sailed instantly into the air, shouting with glee.

"Come on!" called Sky Dance. "We only have a few minutes to cover as much ground as we can!"

Sky Dance fluttered away, with Shimmer Leaf behind her. Addie looked at her sister and motioned for the two of them to follow.

As they took off, the queen, king, and other butterflies soared into the air, too. Addie caught a glimpse of them, flying together in a burst of beautiful color. All that fluttering made its own warm breeze, surrounding Addie and filling her with joy.

Addie and Clara flew side by side. Clara started laughing. "This is amazing!"

It was true. Addie had never felt more free . . . or more herself. It seemed completely natural that she was a butterfly, flapping her wings, feeling the air *whoosh* by her and even through her.

But they had work to do.

"Keep your eyes peeled for Tiger Streak!" shouted Sky Dance from up ahead.

"And your ears!" added Shimmer Leaf.

The four butterflies zoomed ahead of the group and through the grove, weaving in and out of the twisty branches of the giant Changing Tree. Sky Dance led them toward the creek. Addie could see the lemon-yellow crickets gathered on the bank, and even hear their music drifting up into the air.

"Addie and Clara, fly right along the creek!" called Sky Dance. "Shimmer and I will spread out in the trees on the other side. Send us a message if you see Tiger Streak!"

Sky Dance and Shimmer Leaf headed off in another direction, while Addie and Clara flew down the middle of the creek as if it were a road. Addie scanned one side, while Clara searched the other.

Addie knew they didn't have much time as butterflies. Maybe only a few more seconds . . .

"Look!" yelled Clara. "Up ahead!"

Addie saw a fallen tree lying across the creek, and on that tree were two clusters of color. Black, yellow, orange.

"It's them!" shouted Addie. "Come on!"

Addie and Clara flapped their wings as fast as they could, aiming for an expert landing next to Tiger Streak and the bee. They were almost there.

Then, colors filled Addie's eyes again. Sparkles like on the Fourth of July.

"No!" she cried.

Splash.

Addie suddenly felt very wet and very cool, bubbles frothing around her.

She'd landed in the water. Her wings were gone, and she was big again. Her human hands and feet sank into the soft mud at the creek bottom . . . and she couldn't pull them out.

She was completely stuck.

CHAPTER THREE

W owie zowie!" muttered Clara, breathless. She'd plopped right into the creek, too.

"I think my hands and feet are trapped!" yelled Addie. She tugged harder, but the mud seemed to be tugging back.

Clara stood up and made her way to Addie. She wrapped her arms under her sister's, then pulled her up. Addie's hands broke free, then her feet.

"Thanks!" said Addie. "Are you okay?"

Clara nodded. Together, they made their way to the creek bank. The blue water swirled around their ankles, and Addie spied tiny pink fish just under the surface.

When they got to dry land, the girls sat on a rock and took off their sneakers, squeezing them out.

"Are Tiger Streak and the bee still there?" Addie whispered to Clara. "Can you see them?"

Clara craned her neck toward the fallen tree, then nodded. "They're still there. Lucky they didn't see us."

"Okay, good. Why don't you go talk to them? Move slowly. Let them know you're a friend."

"Just me?" asked Clara. "Shouldn't we go together?" Addie could tell her sister was both surprised and annoyed. It was a look Addie called "surpannoyed."

"Uh, well," mumbled Addie, "I was thinking that maybe the sight of two humans might scare them."

"And also, you're afraid of bees," teased Clara.

Addie felt her face flush. "That too."

"Come on, Addie. Yesterday, you let gigantic wasps chase you! That bee is nothing in comparison!"

"True . . . ," said Addie, but she wasn't quite convinced.

"Oh no!" said Clara suddenly, pointing. "They're flying away!"

Addie turned to look. Tiger Streak and the bee were in the air, but only briefly, before landing on a stone in the creek. It was a spot not far from where the girls had fallen. The two girls listened closely and could hear them talking.

"*Bzzz!*" said Tiger Streak. "I know I saw something over here! And heard something!"

"Don't worry about that right now," said the bee. "We have to get you back."

"Yes! Back to the hive! They'll notice two of their bees missing, for sure!"

Clara turned to look at Addie with wide eyes and whispered, "Tiger Streak thinks she's a bee! That's why she's making that noise!"

"It must be the enchantment," said Addie. "I'm sure that bee had something to do with it, too."

Bzzz! Bzzz!

Now Tiger Streak and the bee were

flying again, headed to the other side of the creek.

"Addie! Clara!" came Sky Dance's voice. The girls turned to see their butterfly friends zipping toward them.

"We just saw Tiger Streak," said Clara.

"And we know where she's going," added Addie. She explained that Tiger Streak must have woken up thinking she was a bee, thanks to the enchantment, and was being led back to a hive.

Sky Dance and Shimmer Leaf exchanged a confused look. Their dark eyes grew extra wide. "That doesn't make sense," said Shimmer Leaf. "The bees have always been our friends."

"All of them?" asked Addie. "Maybe these are a new group of bees."

"That's possible," said Sky Dance.

"Mother knows where all the hives are in these woods. We should go back and talk to her."

Clara jumped up. "Oh!"

"What's wrong?" asked Addie.

"I told Mom we were going for a walk, remember? She told us not to be gone long. But we totally have been! We were supposed to come back to eat!"

"It's okay," said Addie. "We'll go now." Addie hated to leave Wishing Wing Grove while there was still helping to do, but she also didn't want her mother to worry. What if she came looking for them in the woods?

Sky Dance must have read her mind. "I'll send a message as soon as I find out where all the nearby hives are," she said to Addie. "Then we can visit each one."

The butterflies led Addie and Clara out of Wishing Wing Grove, then through Silk Meadow. From there, Sky Dance and Shimmer Leaf flew off to find Rose Glow, and the girls rushed through the woods toward home. As they got closer, Addie heard Mom calling their names.

"We're here!" shouted Addie as they ran into the yard.

Mom's jaw dropped. "You were in the woods?"

"Yup," said Addie.

"The woods you're terrified of?"

"They're not terrifying anymore!" said Clara. "They're filled with—"

Addie kicked the back of Clara's leg. She didn't think Clara would blab about the butterflies, but she'd been known to spill the beans before. A reminder couldn't hurt.

"They're filled with really cool things to explore," continued Addie.

"Told you so," said Mom with a smile. "You girls ran out before breakfast. Have some lunch. You'll need energy for more exploring."

"Thanks, Mom!" said Addie.

She and Clara ran into the kitchen, grabbed a box of cereal and a carton of milk, then came back outside to sit on the steps of the deck. Addie ate straight from the cereal box with a spoon while Clara drank some milk. Then they switched.

"So," said Addie. "We were butterflies for a few minutes."

"It was incredible," sighed Clara.

"Your wings were beautiful."

Clara smiled. "So were yours."

"With any luck, we'll get to do that again soon."

They were quiet for several moments, while Clara munched and Addie listened to the sounds of their neighborhood. Mom in the kitchen, running the sink faucet. An airplane flying somewhere overhead. The creak of a swing next door . . .

Next door!

Addie jumped up and ran to the tall bushes that divided their yard from Morgan's. She peeked through a bare spot in the branches and saw Morgan pushing herself on the swing.

"What are you doing?" asked Clara, coming up behind Addie.

"That's Morgan, our next-door neighbor," said Addie. "I met her this morning.

Then I was sort of . . . rude. But not on purpose! When we were talking, Sky Dance called and I had to come find you."

"She still looks pretty upset. Maybe you should go apologize."

"Tomorrow," said Addie, feeling embarrassed about what happened. She began to walk back toward the house, but Clara grabbed her arm and pulled her through the bushes toward Morgan's yard.

"Hi!" shouted Clara, waving to Morgan. "I'm Clara!"

Addie wriggled away from Clara, but

it was too late. Morgan had seen her. She stopped swinging and stared at them.

"Hi, Clara," said Morgan.

Clara walked toward Morgan. *Nooo!* thought Addie, but she had no choice but to follow her sister. Clara had always been better at meeting new people. Awkward situations didn't seem to horrify her the way they did everyone else.

"That's a cool swing set," said Clara.

"Thanks," said Morgan. "I have to stay out here until I'm ready to apologize to my brother for ruining his ball."

Clara looked confused, so Addie decided to explain. "Morgan turned a soccer ball into a face. It was really awesome."

Morgan glanced up at Addie and smiled for a second. Addie got the sense that Morgan didn't usually get compliments on her "art."

Then Addie took a deep breath and swallowed hard.

"Hey," she said to Morgan. "I want to apologize about earlier. I didn't mean to run off like that, but . . . well, I realized there was something important I had to do. I'd love to talk to you more and get the scoop on our neighborhood."

Morgan smiled again. "That would be fun," she said. "But right now I'm supposed to be feeling sorry about what I did. Maybe later?"

"Later is good," said Addie.

The girls said goodbye to one another. Addie and Clara pushed their way back through the bushes to their own yard.

"She's nice," whispered Clara to Addie. "But she also seems kind of sad."

Sad. Just like Clara had been, only a day before. When she'd really needed a wish.

"Clara!" said Addie. "Of course! Morgan is just the person we need! If we can get her to catch and release Tiger Streak, then Tiger Streak can grant her a wish! If only we knew where that buzzing butterfly was . . ."

"Well, that's easy," said Clara.

"What do you mean?" asked Addie.

Clara rolled her eyes and pointed. "Duh! Tiger Streak's right over there."

CHAPTER FOUR

Tiger Streak was hard to miss.

She was resting on a tree. Her yellow-, orange-, and black-striped wings were so bright they seemed electric. They were like little colored lights flickering on the tree's trunk.

It was also hard to miss the silly *bzzz* sound she was making.

Addie watched as the bee landed on

the tree next to Tiger Streak. She pulled Clara around to the side of the house so they wouldn't be spotted.

"If they start flying again, let's follow them," whispered Addie to Clara. "Maybe the hive is nearby."

"It is!" shouted a familiar voice. Sky Dance landed on Addie's arm.

"We must try to catch that bee before he can lead Tiger Streak there!" added Shimmer Leaf, settling onto what must be her favorite spot on Clara's shoulder. "We think their plan is to keep her until sunset, when she loses her magic."

"We found a girl who needs a wish," said Addie. "She lives right next door."

"Excellent!" said Sky Dance.

"But how do we catch a bee?" Addie asked. The thought of getting anywhere near it gave her the willies.

"Don't humans have those thingama-jigs?" asked Sky Dance. "On long sticks? We call them The Terrorizers."

"Oh!" said Addie. "You mean butterfly nets!"

"That sounds even worse!" said Sky Dance.

"We don't have any," said Clara. "Where we used to live in the city, we didn't go around catching butterflies for fun."

"Normally, I'd be relieved to hear that," said Shimmer Leaf, "if we didn't need one right now."

Sky Dance left Addie's arm and joined Shimmer Leaf on Clara's shoulder. "Shimmer?" she asked, putting her furry pink head close to her sister's. "You know . . . we can, um, make one."

Shimmer Leaf paused for a moment,

then burst out laughing. "Silly me! Of course! I keep forgetting that I can do magic!"

"It's okay," said Sky Dance, tapping a reassuring wing to Shimmer's. "You're still getting used to being a Wishing Wing." The butterfly turned to Addie and Clara. "Can you help? You know how our powers of metamorphosis work. We can change one thing into another, but it has to be . . ."

"Connected somehow," finished Addie. "I get it."

"Do we have *any* kind of net in the house?" asked Clara.

"I don't think so," replied Addie. She thought hard. *What does a net do? It catches things, but lets other things through—like air or water.* Surely they owned something that fit the bill . . .

Then a picture popped into her head.

"Be right back!" she exclaimed.

Addie ran into the house, opened a kitchen drawer, and started shuffling through. She hoped and hoped that her mother had already unpacked the item she was picturing. But it wasn't there.

"Argh!" she shouted, frustrated. Any second, Tiger Streak and the bee would start flying again, and they had to be ready to chase them. She rushed to a stack of boxes in the corner of the kitchen. She opened the box on top and started rummaging through it. Finally, at the very bottom of the box, Addie found what she was looking for.

It was a small strainer with a handle. Basically, a net! Except metal, and with very small openings. Addie sometimes used it when she helped her mom boil eggs in water. They'd empty the whole pot into the strainer. The strainer "caught" the eggs, but let the water drain through.

Once, in their old apartment, she'd seen her father trap a spider with it, then slide a piece of paper under the spider and bring it to the open windowsill, where they set it free.

Addie ran outside with the strainer and put it on the ground for Sky Dance, Shimmer Leaf, and Clara to see.

"Will this work?" asked Addie, breathless.

"Yes, indeed!" laughed Sky Dance. "I can see the connection!"

"Can I do it?" asked Shimmer Leaf. "I need the practice."

Sky Dance nodded, and Shimmer Leaf began flying in a neat circle around the strainer. She left a shimmering trail of purple, peach, and mint green as she went. Once, twice, three times she flew in that circle. A cloud of colored dust rose up from the ground.

When that dust settled, there was a butterfly net in the strainer's place. The whole thing was shiny silver that sparkled in the light.

"I was aiming to make a net that I wouldn't mind being caught in!" exclaimed Shimmer Leaf proudly. "And I do think I succeeded!"

Clara grabbed the net and waved it around. "Perfect!" she laughed.

"Look!" shouted Sky Dance, who had

flown to peek around the corner of the house. "They're on the move!"

They all followed Sky Dance. Addie saw Tiger Streak and the bee flying away from the tree. Sky Dance started chasing, and Shimmer Leaf followed close behind. Clara and Addie ran as fast as they could.

There was no time to get turned into a butterfly. *But maybe*, thought Addie, *I can tap into that butterfly spirit*. She let the memory of soaring through the air fill her head, and it felt like that memory was also powering her legs and arms and feet. Addie ran faster.

Up ahead, Addie could see Tiger Streak and the bee zigzagging toward their driveway.

They knew they were being chased now. No question about that.

The pair flew a wide loop around

Mom's car, then down the driveway and around the mailbox. Clara caught up to Sky Dance and Shimmer Leaf, but still wasn't close enough to use the net.

Back up the driveway, across the front lawn, and *boom boom boom* up the stairs to the front porch they all went. Tiger Streak flew in tiny loops, clearly terrified.

For a moment, the bee was close enough to catch.

SWISH!

Clara reached for it with the net, but missed.

Now Tiger Streak and the bee dashed across the porch, then around the side of the house toward the backyard again.

When they rounded the corner of the house to the backyard, Addie realized she'd left the door open. She watched

with horror as the bee led Tiger Streak right into the house!

Clara, Addie, and both Wishing Wings followed.

Pepper ran into the kitchen. He barked, saw all the flying things, and started chasing, too.

Great, thought Addie. *Here comes Mom any second now.*

But she heard loud music coming from upstairs. Mom was unpacking again, listening to the radio.

They all thundered through the kitchen, around the brand-new dining room table, and into the living room. When the bee led the chase toward the hallway, Addie thought, *Not upstairs! Please not upstairs!*

She let out a sigh of relief when the bee zipped right past the stairway and into the family room. Tiger Streak *bzzzed* up and down, back and forth.

"Tiger Streak, don't be frightened!" shouted Sky Dance. "It's not you we're trying to catch! It's the bee!"

"We're trying to help you!" added Shimmer Leaf.

At that, the bee slowed down. It seemed surprised.

Clara was right underneath it. Addie saw her reach up and steady the net.

Clara brought it down to the floor quickly, shouting, "I got it! I got it!"

Addie rushed to see. There was something frantically jumping around inside the net, for sure.

She felt a *whoosh* by her ear.

Addie looked up just in time to glimpse Tiger Streak flitting past her, into the kitchen and out through the open door.

CHAPTER FIVE

Addie glanced down at the very unhappy bee in the net and felt herself go into panic mode. The bee was buzzing so loudly that she was sure it was making the walls vibrate.

Pepper ran circles around the net, barking, but Clara shooed him away.

"Addie, do something!" she called. "Put the dog somewhere!"

Addie snapped herself out of it. She was happy to do anything that meant getting away from the bee. She scooped up Pepper and locked him in the downstairs bathroom. *He'll be mad*, thought Addie, *but I'd rather deal with an angry Pepper than an angry bee.*

When she came back, Clara was kneeling on the floor, her face close to the bee in the net. Sky Dance and Shimmer Leaf sat on each of Clara's shoulders.

"Did you just say something?" Clara asked the bee.

Addie moved closer, but not too close.

"Yes!" said the bee, sounding frantic and frightened. Addie could tell from his voice that he was a boy. "I said, please let me go! I'm trying to help Tiger Streak too!"

Clara glanced up at Addie, then at the

two butterflies. Each butterfly shook her wings in a kind of shrug. Clara narrowed her eyes and leaned in closer to the bee. "What exactly do you mean?"

The bee landed and let out one long, frustrated *bzzz*. Then he took a deep breath and spoke again, this time more slowly.

"When you told Tiger Streak you have to keep her safe from the bees—you were right about that. There's a whole swarm of them coming to take her to our hive!"

"Isn't that what *you* were doing?" asked Sky Dance.

"No!" cried the bee, and he threw himself against the net again.

"I don't believe him!" said Shimmer Leaf. "I bet he's trying to trick us!"

"Wait, Shimmer," said Sky Dance, dipping her antennae toward the bee.

"I think we should give him a chance to explain."

The bee sighed. "Thank you!"

"What's your name?" asked Clara.

"I'm Kirby."

"Kirby," continued Clara, "why were you with Tiger Streak in Wishing Wing Grove?"

Kirby took another deep breath. Addie drew two steps closer, to make sure she could hear what he was saying. She could see his fuzzy face and black-and-yellow-striped body. Now that he was calm, he didn't seem so scary anymore. He was actually rather . . . cute.

"This morning," Kirby began, "our queen called a hive meeting and told us that the Wishing Wings are our enemies. She didn't tell us why! She just said we were supposed to hate them from now on. So all the bees in our colony started saying bad stuff about the butterflies, and how they never liked them anyway."

"That's awful!" exclaimed Clara.

"They can't really help it," said Kirby sadly. "It's their job to just do, and think, whatever the queen tells them."

"Do you think that, too?" asked Shimmer Leaf.

Kirby puffed out his little striped chest and shook his head. "No, I don't. I've always been kind of . . . well, they call me weird. Because I tend to think for myself. It's a bad habit."

"That's a *good* habit!" said Clara.

"Not for a bee," muttered Kirby. "I get teased all the time. But still, I couldn't help it. When the queen announced that the butterflies hated us and we should hate them back, I wanted some proof. I flew to Wishing Wing Grove, and that's where I found Tiger Streak acting like a bee. I could tell there was something terribly wrong. I know a dark enchantment when I see one. I tried to explain to her that she's a butterfly, but she wouldn't listen. I kept trying, though. I kept following her."

Addie thought back to everything she'd seen in the grove. It did seem like Kirby was flying *behind* Tiger Streak. Maybe he was telling the truth.

"So you weren't leading her to a hive?"

Addie asked. She took one step closer, then stopped.

Kirby's huge, round black eyes looked Addie up and down. "No! I was trying to bring her to your queen and king."

Addie took a step back, and Kirby tilted his head at her.

"You're afraid of me, aren't you?" he asked, sounding hurt. "I can see it on your face."

"Don't mind her," said Clara. "She's afraid of anything with a stinger."

"You got hurt once," said Kirby to Addie. His voice was gentle and understanding.

"I stepped on a wasp," she replied.

Kirby nodded. "You hurt it first. By accident, of course. But that's why it hurt you back. It was afraid. We don't sting without a reason. We're not meanies like that."

"We need the bees," added Sky Dance. "They spread pollen between plants and flowers. Without them, many things wouldn't grow!"

"Don't be frightened of us," said Kirby. "The other bees think it's funny when humans are scared, but I hate being misunderstood that way."

Addie thought about that. Since yesterday, she had overcome her fear of the woods, faced down gigantic wasps, and even tried to meet a new friend. Maybe it was time to tackle this fear, too. She took one, two, then three steps, and now her feet were right at the net. She knelt down to get a good look at Kirby. Up close, he really was adorable.

"What do you think, Addie?" asked

Sky Dance, who had landed on Addie's arm. "If he's telling the truth, he could lead us to Tiger Streak."

Addie considered that, then motioned for Clara and the butterflies to follow her into the living room. This way, they could talk in private.

"I believe him," said Clara.

Sky Dance nodded. "Mama always says, assume that someone's heart is good."

Addie turned to Shimmer Leaf. "That's two votes. What about you?"

Shimmer Leaf thought for a few moments, then finally nodded. "I vote yes."

"Me too," said Addie. She led them back into the kitchen, then bent down close to Kirby.

"We're going to let you go," she told him.

"Good choice!" Kirby exclaimed. "Because I just saw the swarm outside! The queen told them to bring Tiger Streak back to our hive, but I know how to throw them off her trail."

Addie grabbed the handle of the net, took a deep breath, and lifted it up. She crossed her fingers that she wasn't going to regret this.

Kirby zoomed into the air, landed for a second on Addie's nose, and gave her what felt like a bee hug.

"Thanks!" he cried.

Addie let out a laugh. Bee hugs tickle! Then Kirby darted out the door to the deck. Addie closed the door, and they all hid behind it.

"There's the swarm!" said Clara, peeking through the window of the door.

Addie saw what appeared to be a

thick, dark, moving cloud in their backyard. The cloud was made of flying bees!
Her first thought was *ewwww*, but as she
watched the bees fly so close, mirroring
one another's movements, she had to
admit it was also pretty cool.

Kirby raced toward the swarm and
landed on the deck railing.

"Have you seen the New Bloom?"
asked the swarm in unison. Their voices
together sounded like a creepy chorus.

"Yes!" shouted Kirby. "She was captured by a human girl with red hair and
taken inside a house!" He was doing a
good job of pretending to be upset. "We
can't get to her anymore!" he continued.
"I'm so mad!"

"Captured?" echoed the swarm. "By a
human? We have strict orders not to let
that happen! 'Find the New Bloom, bring

her here. Don't let any humans catch her.' That's what the queen said."

"I know, I was there," said Kirby, rolling his shiny black eyes. "I tried to stop her, but the human had a net."

The swarm hummed for a few moments, as if it were thinking. "We must find the girl with red hair!" it announced.

"You do that," said Kirby. "I'll stay here in case she comes back!"

The swarm changed from a round shape to a long, airplane-like shape, then flew away. When the bees were safely out of sight, Addie, Clara, and the butterflies stepped out onto the deck.

Kirby was laughing. "Ha! Did you see that! They just believed whatever I told them!"

"Why did you tell them Tiger Streak

was captured by a girl with red hair?" asked Clara.

"I wanted to keep them away from you two. *You* have dark honey hair," he said, pointing an antenna at Clara. "*You* have light honey hair," he continued, pointing the other antenna at Addie. "The swarm will leave you alone. They'll fly around the neighborhood and find no human girl. They'll go back to the hive and report their failure to the queen. They give up easily. It's really embarrassing."

"Nice trick!" said Sky Dance.

"Then we'll be free to search for Tiger Streak without them bothering us," Kirby added.

Addie smiled. Kirby *was* tricky, but in a good way. She thought of the swarm buzzing around the neighborhood, looking in vain for a girl with red hair.

A girl with red hair . . .

An image of Morgan popped into Addie's head.

Morgan . . . and her red hair!

"Oh my gosh!" shouted Addie. "We've got to go!"

CHAPTER SIX

Addie rushed toward Morgan's yard.
Yikes, she thought. *This friendship is REALLY getting off on the wrong foot.*

"Addie!" shouted Clara, running up beside her. "What's wrong?"

"Morgan has red hair," replied Addie. "If the swarm finds her, they'll think she's the one who caught Tiger Streak!"

Clara stopped dead. "Oh. Oops."

"I'm such a dummy!" cried Kirby, who was whizzing by over their heads.

"It's okay," said Addie. "We have to find her anyway. She needs a wish. She's the one who can catch Tiger Streak and break her enchantment!"

They stepped through the bushes, and Addie scanned Morgan's yard. The swing set was empty. In the far corner of the yard, there was a garden bordered on two sides by a stone wall. The garden had definitely seen better days. A few limp flowers struggled to stand up straight, and everything else was brown and shriveled. A small wooden playhouse sat next to the garden, looking forgotten and unused.

Sky Dance and Shimmer Leaf flew into the playhouse, then reappeared.

"Nothing in there except a lot of cobwebs," said Shimmer Leaf.

"We should see if she's in the house," said Clara.

Sky Dance, Shimmer Leaf, and Kirby hid themselves behind the garden wall. Addie took a deep breath, stepped up to a bright red door at the back of the house, and knocked.

After a few moments, Mrs. Werner answered.

"Oh, hi!" she said, with a friendly smile. "Addie, right?"

"Yes. This is my sister, Clara."

Clara waved. Mrs. Werner waved back.

"Is, um, Morgan home?" asked Addie.

"She was," said Mrs. Werner. "For about two minutes, when she finally came inside and apologized to her brother about his ball." She sighed. "Then she grabbed her scooter and said she was going for a ride around the neighborhood."

Addie pictured Morgan riding her scooter alone, right into the path of the bee swarm. She felt herself go back into panic mode.

"Okay, thanks!" she called to Mrs. Werner. "Got to go!" She grabbed Clara and they started running away.

Great, thought Addie. *Now I've been rude to Morgan AND her mom.*

Clara and Addie ran down Morgan's driveway and stopped at the street. They waited for Sky Dance, Shimmer Leaf, and Kirby to catch up to them.

"We heard," said Sky Dance as she landed on Morgan's mailbox. It was painted with a big yellow sun, and Addie knew instantly it was Morgan's artwork. "Let's find her."

"I guess it's our turn to get a tour of Brook Forest," added Shimmer Leaf as she and Kirby came to rest on the mailbox as well.

"That might be a problem," said Addie. "We don't know our way around."

"We've only been to the end of our driveway," admitted Clara.

Sky Dance folded up her wings and gave Addie a look of disbelief. "You mean you haven't explored your neighborhood *at all*?" she asked.

"We just moved here!" said Addie.

"Mom kept wanting us to go for a walk, but Addie was too nervous about all the nature," said Clara. "And I was still too sad."

Sky Dance shook her head, but she was smiling. "Well, I guess now's the time."

"I'll go find Tiger Streak," said Kirby. "She trusts me. I'll meet you back at Morgan's house."

After Kirby flew off, Addie, Clara, and the butterflies set off quickly down the street. So far, Addie had only seen her new road from the car. Now that she was walking, she noticed things she hadn't before. The way the trees arched their branches over the road like a canopy. The pretty sky-blue color of the house next to Morgan's. When they reached the house after that, Addie could hear laughter and the sounds of splashing. A swimming pool!

After a few minutes, the street dead-ended onto another. Should they go right or left?

"I wish we had a map," said Addie. "It would be great to get a bird's-eye view of this place."

Sky Dance laughed. "You don't need a bird's-eye view, silly. You have a butterfly's eye view!"

"Oh," said Addie, laughing too. "Duh."

"Come on, Shimmer," shouted Sky Dance as the Wishing Wings soared into the air. As they went higher, they appeared smaller. From this distance, Addie couldn't even see their colors. They looked like ordinary butterflies.

Addie and Clara waited anxiously. After a minute, the butterflies fluttered back toward them.

"The street goes in a big circle!" reported Shimmer Leaf.

"We saw Morgan! She went that way!" added Sky Dance, pointing a wing to the right. "We saw the swarm, too. They went to the left. In a minute or two, they'll run smack-dab into each other."

"Come on," said Clara, turning right. Addie and the butterflies followed.

As the road started to curve, Addie could see Morgan up ahead, the bright colors of her bike helmet bobbing along.

"Morgan!" shouted Addie.

But they were too far away, and Morgan couldn't hear them.

"We won't catch up to her. She's on a scooter!"

"I have an idea," said Clara, tapping her finger on her chin. "You said the street goes in a big circle?"

"Yes," said Sky Dance.

Clara pointed at a green house on their left. "If we cut through that yard and the one behind it, we'll reach the other side of the circle more quickly. We can find Morgan before the swarm does."

"Good thinking!" whooped Shimmer Leaf.

But the thought of this made Addie cringe. "Clara, no," she said. "We're supposed to be meeting new neighbors, not barging through their property!"

"This is kind of an emergency! Besides, we'll go fast. Maybe they won't even notice."

"It's now or never," said Sky Dance.

Clara didn't wait for Addie to agree. She took off across the lawn of the green house, the butterflies flitting behind her. Addie had no choice but to follow.

They ran around the green house and into the backyard. It was filled with gnome statues. Big gnomes, small gnomes, gnome families . . . even gnome animals.

Addie almost tripped over a gnome rabbit wearing a pointy red hat.

Past that yard, there was a thicket of trees. Then, another yard. In the middle of that yard, a teenage girl lay on a blanket with her headphones on. Her eyes were closed, and she was bopping her head to music. Addie and Clara sped right past her.

Just as Clara had predicted, once they ran around that house, they found themselves back on the street . . . on the other side of the loop.

They looked left. There was the bee swarm.

They looked right. Here came Morgan on her scooter.

"Morgan!" shouted Addie, stepping directly in front of her.

Morgan skidded her scooter to a stop

and stared at them. Her long red braid peeked out of her helmet, which she'd painted with orange, yellow, and black stripes.

"Quick!" said Clara. "Tuck your hair into your helmet! Don't ask why, we'll explain later."

Morgan must have seen how panicked Addie was, so she grabbed her braid and pushed it up under the edge of the helmet.

The swarm was upon them now.

It stopped and hovered, buzzing in that creepy chorus. It moved toward Addie, then Clara, then Morgan, pausing for a moment or two above each girl. Addie held her breath.

Then the swarm continued on, down the street.

"Phew!" burst out Addie with a sigh of relief.

"Weird," said Morgan as she watched the swarm travel away from them.

There was an awkward pause. Addie glanced up to see Sky Dance and Shimmer Leaf high in the sky above.

"I love the way you painted your helmet," said Clara to Morgan, breaking the silence.

"Thanks," said Morgan. "My mom got mad at me for it, but I think this looks better than just plain white."

"We have boring helmets, too," said Addie. "Will you help us paint them?" She hoped this would be a good way to get Morgan home to her backyard.

Morgan smiled. "Yes! As long as your mom says it's okay."

"Don't worry," replied Addie. "We'll ask."

Once they all got to Morgan's backyard, Addie looked around. Where was Kirby? How long would it take him to find Tiger Streak?

Then, out of the corner of her eye, Addie saw a quick blink of orange. Then another blink of yellow. She heard an unmistakable fake-buzzing. Tiger Streak! She was fluttering near the bushes, with Kirby flying circles around her.

"Hey!" said Addie, giving Clara a nudge. "Look at that beautiful butterfly!"

Clara got the hint and spotted Tiger Streak, too. "Oh! Pretty!" she added, pointing.

Morgan glanced up, saw Tiger Streak, and said, "Wow! That's so cool!"

"Let's try to catch it," said Clara. She ran through the bushes toward their yard, then reappeared a few moments later with the net. Clara offered it to Morgan. "You go first."

Morgan shook her head. "My mom loves butterflies. She'd be mad if she knew I caught one."

"We won't hurt it," said Addie. "We'll just admire it for a minute, then let it go."

"We can take a picture of the butterfly," suggested Clara. "Then you could paint it."

Morgan paused, then smiled. "I like

that idea! I know exactly where to paint it, too."

She took the net. Addie and Clara exchanged a look. *This might work!*

Kirby left the tree and Tiger Streak followed him. They flew toward the girls, and Addie could hear Tiger Streak's buzzing get louder.

"This way!" Kirby shouted to Tiger Streak. "The queen told us we have to go this way!"

Kirby led Tiger Streak right toward Morgan. As the butterfly got closer, Morgan waved the net.

Tiger Streak was trapped inside. Morgan had caught her!

"Yes!" shouted Addie.

Just as a big, dark shadow moved over them.

CHAPTER SEVEN

It was a shadow that hummed and changed shape.

"The swarm!" shouted Clara.

When Morgan saw the bees, she jumped back and dropped the net. Tiger Streak broke free, darting away in a blur of colors.

Addie tried to see which way Tiger Streak went, but the air around her was thick with flying things, buzzing in her ear. She covered her head and started swatting at them. Clara and Morgan did the same. But it all just made the bees more furious. They grew louder, flew faster, and Addie braced herself to feel a sting . . .

"Addie!" Kirby was whispering in her ear. "Remember what I said? Bees will only hurt you if you hurt them first."

Addie nodded and shouted to the others. "Don't fight them! Let's get inside somewhere!" She saw Sky Dance and Shimmer Leaf flying to Morgan's playhouse. *This way!* Sky Dance told her in a thought message.

Addie led Morgan and Clara into the playhouse.

"Blech!" cried Clara, wiping a cobweb off her face.

"Sorry," said Morgan. "I haven't been here in a while."

Addie reached out to close the door behind them. One of its hinges was broken, so it didn't close all the way, but it was good enough. The girls huddled together on the floor. Outside, the sound of the swarm swelled and reminded Addie of raindrops, beating hard against a window.

"What do they want?" cried Morgan.

The humming paused and the swarm was silent for a moment. Then, in that single, eerie voice, it said, "The butterfly! We want the butterfly!"

Morgan gave Addie and Clara a look of alarm. "Did those bees just . . . talk to us?"

"We don't have her!" shouted Clara to the bees. "We did, but she flew away!"

"If we don't bring her the butterfly," said the bees, "she'll be very angry!"

"Tell that queen of yours she can't have Tiger Streak!" said Addie.

"And she should stop saying bad things about our friends!" added Clara.

Morgan simply sat there, looking very confused.

"Not the queen," said the swarm. "The other. The other will be angry!"

"The other?" asked Addie. "Who do you mean?"

"The one who acts like the queen of the queen!" said the swarm.

"Who's *that*?" yelled Addie. She felt as confused as Morgan must have been.

The swarm was silent for a moment, then its shadow slid away from the door.

"They left!" said Clara.

"You just had a conversation with a swarm of bees," said Morgan, shaking her head as if to wake herself up.

Sky Dance poked her little face into the crack along the doorway. "It's safe! You can come out now!"

Sky Dance disappeared. Morgan's jaw dropped open. "A talking butterfly, too?" she asked.

"We'll explain in a minute," said Addie. She pushed open the playhouse door onto the most glorious garden she'd ever seen.

The dry, brown plants were gone. They'd been replaced with dozens of flowers, nearly twinkling in the sunshine. They were purple, red, green, yellow, orange, blue, and quite a few shades in between. Two or three bees perched on each flower, happily drawing nectar.

"Not bad, right?" asked Sky Dance proudly as she hovered over the scene. "It was Kirby's idea to work some magic on the dead flowers. He knew it would distract the swarm."

Morgan stepped into the garden and looked around, her eyes wide.

"Talking bees and butterflies," she said after a few speechless moments. "My mom's depressing garden turned into *this.* Are we . . . are we talking the M-word here?"

Addie smiled. There was only one M-word, as far as she was concerned. "Could be," she said, in a way that meant *yes!*

She and Morgan were going to be good friends, Addie just knew it.

"This is great," said Clara, "but we still have to find our missing New Bloom!"

"No need for that," said a small voice from above. Something fluttered out of the air and landed on Morgan's arm.

"Tiger Streak!" exclaimed Sky Dance.

"That's me," said the butterfly. "But how did I get here? I don't even remember coming out of my chrysalis."

"You were under an enchantment," explained Shimmer Leaf. "But Morgan broke it by catching you, then setting you free."

Morgan lifted her arm so she and Tiger Streak were staring straight into each other's eyes.

"Hi," said Morgan, smiling. "We have the same style." She pointed to her orange-, yellow-, and black-painted helmet.

"Looks like I was truly meant to be your Wishing Wing!" laughed Tiger

Streak. "And now I get to grant you a wish."

"A wish," echoed Morgan.

"Choose carefully," added Tiger Streak. "You get just one."

Morgan bit her lip. "There are so many things to wish for. How does anyone choose?"

"Imagine the thing that will make you the happiest right now," suggested Addie. "That worked for me and Clara."

Morgan stared off at the garden, where Kirby and the bees were still having their own little nectar party.

"Oh!" she exclaimed, and walked past the flowers to the rock wall. Tiger Streak fluttered into the air to follow her. There were large stones and planks of wood covering one section of the wall. Morgan began removing them. Then she stepped back.

Part of the wall was painted with flowers. Morgan's work, for sure. They were as colorful as the real ones in the garden now, but smudged and messy. It was clear that Morgan kept making mistakes and trying to fix them. A few unfinished flowers had stems, but no blooms.

"I was trying to make this mural for my mom," said Morgan. "She got frustrated with the garden and gave up on it. I thought, if I could give her flowers some other way, maybe she'd finally see why I paint things that she doesn't think should be painted."

Morgan turned to Tiger Streak and took a deep breath.

"I wish . . . I wish my mom understood me and my art. Is that silly?"

"Not silly at all. Everyone wants to be understood," said Addie. She and Kirby exchanged a glance.

Tiger Streak flitted back and forth across the wall, examining the painted flowers. "I know just what to do!" she said. "But you should step back!"

Morgan went to stand next to Addie.

"Watch this," said Addie, nudging Morgan with her elbow.

Tiger Streak flew three wide circles around the wall. Glittering ribbons of orange, yellow, and black unrolled behind her. Morgan gasped at the sight of it.

When Tiger Streak was done, and the colors dissolved into the air, they could all see the result.

The wall looked like a giant painting. There were flowers, grass, a few butterflies . . . and even a bee.

"Oh my gosh," mumbled Morgan. "That's exactly what I was trying to do, but couldn't!"

"Glad I could lend a hand," said Tiger Streak. "Or rather, a wing."

"Morgan?" called a voice.

Startled, the bees flew off into the woods. The girls turned to see Mrs. Werner standing behind them. The butterflies zoomed over to the wall, hiding themselves among the painted flowers.

"What happened here?" Mrs. Werner asked, staring at the wall and garden.

"It's . . . it's a surprise for you," said Morgan.

"You did this?"

Morgan looked hurt. "The wall's ruined, isn't it? I'm sorry. I'm sorry about Calvin's ball and my helmet, and all the other things I painted that I wasn't supposed to. I just want to add some beautiful things to the world."

Mrs. Werner pulled Morgan into a hug.

"I can't believe you brought my garden back to life!" she said.

"Oh," said Morgan. "Right."

"Your mural is fantastic, and I love it. Oh, honey, all you ever had to do was talk to me about how you were feeling."

Morgan smiled big. It was the smile of a wish come true.

❦ ❦ ❦

After Morgan and her mother went inside, Addie and Clara returned to their own yard.

They sat on the steps of the deck, cuddling with Squish. The three Wishing

Wings and Kirby whirled in circles over their heads, riding the breeze.

"Wow!" called Tiger Streak. "It feels amazing to have wings. And look at these stripes! They're as sleek as a tiger's!"

She made a tiger-like roaring noise, followed by a growl.

"No more pretending you're something you're not!" teased Sky Dance, and they all laughed.

"The next time we come to the grove, can we bring Morgan?" asked Clara.

"Oh no," said Sky Dance, growing serious. "She won't remember anything about us. Before we left, we sprinkled Forgetting Magic all over the garden. Morgan will remember that you helped her with the mural, but that's all."

"What about Tiger Streak?" asked

Addie. "Isn't she Morgan's Wishing Wing now? The way Sky Dance is connected to me, and Shimmer is connected to Clara?"

"She is, indeed," Sky Dance replied. "Morgan will feel her butterfly spirit get stronger whenever Tiger Streak is nearby. We have to use Forgetting Magic with most humans, but with you two . . . well, you're special. You were chosen to help us, and you truly have!"

"Hopefully, we'll help you some more," said Addie.

"There are still two more New Blooms under the enchantment," added Clara.

"Yes," said Sky Dance. "And now you know there's a neighborhood filled with children, just like the two of you and Morgan, who need wishes granted."

"Meeting the first new neighbor

wasn't so bad, was it?" said Clara, nudging Addie.

Addie nudged her back. It hadn't been bad at all. Actually, it had been wonderful!

Sky Dance flew up toward the roof of the house so she could peek at the sun's position in the sky. "We need to get home," she said. "Mama will be eager to hear about our adventure, and we have to introduce them to Kirby!"

Kirby flew a loop in the air. "Maybe I'll fit in better with magic butterflies than with a colony of bees who can't think for themselves," he said.

"That reminds me," said Addie. "What do you think the swarm meant about 'the queen of the queen'?"

"I'm not sure," replied Sky Dance. "I suspect the queen bee wasn't the one ordering the colony to capture Tiger Streak. She was being controlled, or influenced, by someone else."

"The same someone who's behind the enchantment!" said Addie.

"Very likely," agreed Sky Dance.

Mew, said Squish, as if he agreed, too. They all laughed.

"I think he's hungry," said Clara. "We should go inside."

"Poor Pepper!" remembered Addie. "He's still locked in the bathroom!"

"It's been a busy day," said Shimmer Leaf.

"A *magically* busy day," corrected Clara.

The sisters waved goodbye to their four flying friends, watching them disappear into the woods beyond the edge of the yard.

As she and Clara headed to the back

door, Addie looked up to see Morgan's face in an upstairs window of her house. She was waving at them. They waved back.

I have a new friend! thought Addie. She remembered what Madame Furia said about other kinds of magic. Friendship was definitely one of them.

Tomorrow, maybe they'd discover some more.

Butterfly Wishes

Blue Rain's Adventure

PROLOGUE

Deep in a wooded grove, there was a jagged rock covered in bright green moss that glistened with morning dew.

A butterfly perched at the very top of the rock. She was staring up at a huge willow tree nearby, nervously fluttering her orange, yellow, and black tiger-striped wings. This was no ordinary butterfly;

this was a Wishing Wing butterfly . . . and she was magic.

"Come on, Tiger Streak!" called another Wishing Wing named Sky Dance, as she flew in circles around the tree trunk. Sky Dance's wings were brilliant pink and turquoise, with cloud patterns on them.

Tiger Streak took a deep breath and shot into the air, following her friend toward the big willow tree. They both landed on the edge of a small hollow in the tree's trunk. Tiger Streak peered into the hollow.

Inside, she saw four gray shapes hanging. Two were the shriveled remains of chrysalides that had once held caterpillars as they transformed into Wishing Wings.

"That was my chrysalis, right?" Tiger Streak asked Sky Dance, pointing to one of these with her antennae. "I remember spinning it."

"Yes," replied Sky Dance, and then she nodded toward the second opened chrysalis. "And that was Shimmer Leaf's."

Now Tiger Streak examined the other two shapes: chrysalides that hadn't

opened yet. New Wishing Wings would pop out any day now . . . or would they?

"These chrysalides should be glowing and gold," said Tiger Streak, "but they look colorless and sad."

"They're under the dark enchantment," Sky Dance explained. "Just like with you and Shimmer Leaf, when they emerge they may not know they have to grant a wish to a human child before sunset in order to earn their magic."

Tiger Streak shook her head sadly. "I still shudder to think how close I came to losing my magic forever and weakening the magic of all Wishing Wings. We have to find out who's behind this!"

"We will," said Sky Dance. "At least, I hope we will. But first we have to see if the next butterfly needs help earning her magic."

"I would say we're about to find out," said Tiger Streak. She pointed an antenna at a chrysalis that was wiggling and jiggling so much, it looked like it was dancing.

As the chrysalis slowly began to open, Sky Dance leaned in close to Tiger Streak and whispered, "Get ready!"

Both butterflies stretched out their wings, strong and straight, prepared for whatever was about to happen next.

CHAPTER ONE

Addie Gibson crouched behind an old woodpile, hugging her knees tight. She tried to breathe as quietly as she could, even though her heart was pounding. Hopefully this hiding place would keep her safe.

Then she heard a voice echo against the trees.

"Twenty-nine, thirty!" yelled Addie's

friend Morgan. "Ready or not, here I come!"

This was a seriously intense round of hide-and-seek.

Addie listened to Morgan's footsteps as they grew fainter, which meant she was walking toward the other side of Addie's backyard. *Phew*, thought Addie. Maybe Morgan would find Addie's sister Clara first.

Addie and Clara had just moved from the city to this house in Brook Forest. They'd known Morgan, their next-door neighbor, for only a day. Addie wanted to show her new friend that even though she wasn't used to playing this game outdoors, she could totally do it. She could ignore the slimy, damp ground underneath her and pretend not to see the spiderweb on the woodpile three inches from her face.

Addie hated spiders. They were so creepy. Whenever one had appeared in her old apartment, she'd screamed for help. If one popped up now, she'd probably do the same.

Then Addie remembered something.

You used to hate bees too, she told herself. *Now you know better.*

It was true. Yesterday they had met a bee named Kirby who was about as nice as anyone she'd ever met, human or insect.

Yes, she'd met a bee. Talked to him. Wasps and caterpillars too. And, of course, BUTTERFLIES! Unique, beautiful, smart, kind, brave butterflies! *Magic* butterflies.

Addie listened to Morgan sneak around the yard. Her footsteps were getting louder and closer, for sure.

It had been two short days since Addie

and Clara discovered Wishing Wing Grove, a secret place deep in the woods behind their new house. The Grove was the home of the enchanted Wishing Wing butterflies, who could do many wonderful things. Like talk, for instance. And grant wishes by turning one thing into another. The sisters had teamed up with two Wishing Wing sisters, Sky Dance and Shimmer Leaf, to help some freshly hatched butterflies known as New Blooms who'd been cursed with a dark enchantment. So far, each New Bloom had needed Addie and Clara's help to break the enchantment and earn its magic by making a wish come true for a human child . . . all before sunset on the day it emerged.

Addie could see the top of Morgan's head as she drew nearer. She prepared herself to be found. Suddenly, there was the sound of an upstairs window opening and Addie's mom's voice.

"Addie, honey! There's someone ringing the doorbell, but I'm on an important call right now. Can you go answer it?"

Addie sighed. Way to ruin a great hiding place! When she popped up from behind the woodpile, she startled Morgan.

"Ahhh!" exclaimed Morgan. "You were right there and I had no idea!"

"See if you can find Clara," said Addie with a smile. Then she sighed. "I have to get the door."

Addie hated answering the door. She never knew who would be there or what she was supposed to say to the person. But she'd done a lot of brave things in the last two days, so maybe it was time to get

over this particular fear. She walked into the house and took a deep breath as she grabbed the handle and pulled, ready to greet a stranger with a big smile on her face.

But nobody was there.

The front porch was empty. Addie stepped out and looked left, then right. Nothing.

She closed the door and turned to find Clara and Morgan standing in the hall behind her. "Who was it?" asked Clara.

Addie opened her mouth to reply. *Ding-dong!* The doorbell rang again.

Clara frowned. "Did you answer it the first time?"

"Yes!"

Now Clara sighed. "Obviously you didn't. I'll get it, because *I'm* not weird that way."

Clara flung open the door.

Nobody was there. Again.

"What . . ." murmured Clara, scanning the porch and steps for any sign of a human being.

Clara was about to close the door when they heard it: a sudden rustling of leaves.

"I know what's going on," whispered Morgan, who had stepped up behind them. "Follow me."

Morgan tiptoed down the porch steps into Addie's front yard, Addie and Clara following behind her. Then Morgan stopped, looked around, and zeroed in on a large bush near the edge of the driveway. She turned to Addie and Clara, pointing to the bush and rolling her eyes.

As Morgan crept toward the bush one silent step at a time, Addie thought,

Whoa, she's good at seeking. Next time I'll find an even better hiding place.

Morgan reached the bush, stuck her arms into it, and pulled apart the branches to reveal . . .

A face.

Which belonged to a very surprised dark-haired boy.

"Got you!" shouted Morgan.

The boy tumbled out of the bush and took off running down the driveway. His blue-and-yellow-striped shirt was a blur as he raced out of sight.

"Who on earth was that?" asked Clara.

Morgan sighed. "That," she said slowly, "was Oliver."

"Does he live on our street?" asked Addie.

"He lives right there," Morgan replied, pointing to the house next door. "We used to be good friends, actually. He used to be *nice*. Now all he does is go around pranking people. We're lucky he didn't have his squirt gun today. He loves sneaking up on kids with that thing!"

"He'd better not ever try to sneak up on me," said Clara.

"I'm sorry you guys aren't friends anymore," Addie said to Morgan.

"I'm sorry too," said Morgan. "It all started when Oliver's big brother James joined the Navy and got stationed overseas. They're super-close and he's basically

Oliver's hero. After he left, Oliver didn't talk to anyone for weeks. Then the pranking started."

Addie thought about what it might feel like for Clara to live so far away. Would she miss her? Probably not at first. She'd celebrate! Nobody to fight with. Nobody to borrow her stuff without asking . . .

"Addie!" Clara burst out, and for a moment Addie worried that Clara could tell what she'd been thinking. But Clara's face was serious, not angry, as she stepped up to whisper in Addie's ear. "I'm getting a thought message from Shimmer Leaf! They need us to come quickly to Wishing Wing Grove!"

Because Shimmer Leaf was Clara's Wishing Wing, they could send thought messages to each other. Sky Dance and Addie were connected the same way.

Addie nodded and closed her eyes, waiting for a message to come from Sky Dance. But there was only silence. That was strange . . .

"It's getting late," said Morgan. "I should get going. I promised my mom I'd help her weed the garden today."

Addie suspected that Tiger Streak, another Wishing Wing, had worked her magic to make Morgan run home. Now Addie and Clara could rush to Wishing Wing Grove without having to explain themselves. Less than twenty-four hours ago, Morgan had helped save Tiger Streak's magic, but afterward, the butterflies had used an enchantment to make Morgan forget it had all happened. Addie felt sad for her new friend, but also knew it was necessary to keep too many humans from discovering Wishing Wing

Grove. Only Addie and Clara were allowed to remember it. Still, Tiger Streak was now officially Morgan's Wishing Wing. Even though Morgan didn't know it, Tiger Streak would always be there, keeping Morgan's butterfly spirit strong.

They said goodbye to Morgan as she headed back home.

"Are you ready?" Addie asked Clara.

"Are you kidding?" Clara replied. "I'm *always* ready."

Addie took her sister's hand. Together they raced toward the line of trees that marked the edge of their backyard—and the beginning of a new adventure.

CHAPTER TWO

Addie and Clara didn't know their way around their neighborhood or town yet, but they knew exactly how to get through the woods to the magical grove. Addie smiled to think about how, just a few days ago, she was afraid to even set foot past her yard.

Eventually, the woods opened up onto a clearing. It was filled with tall green grass that waved in the wind and reminded Addie of an ocean. They had reached Silk Meadow, the entrance to the realm of the Wishing Wings. As they began walking through it, Addie looked at Clara, wondering if her sister felt as excited and nervous as she did.

When the girls were halfway across the meadow, something appeared in the air up ahead. It flew straight for them, growing bigger as it drew nearer. Addie recognized the dancing movement of fluttering wings. Then she spotted the wings' colors: purple, peach, and mint green with leaf patterns. It was Shimmer Leaf! Addie scanned the meadow for Sky Dance, knowing she must not be far behind.

"Wow!" said Shimmer Leaf when

she reached them in the middle of the meadow. "That was fast!"

"We came as soon as I got your message," said Clara.

"Where's Sky Dance?" asked Addie, still searching for her friend.

Shimmer Leaf suddenly looked very sad. She dropped quickly onto Clara's shoulder, her wings folded tight against her body.

"We don't quite know where Sky Dance is," said Shimmer Leaf softly.

Addie felt a *flip-flop* in her stomach. "Is she lost?" she asked.

"Kidnapped?" blurted out Clara. Addie gave her a dirty look. Leave it to Clara to think the worst.

"Nothing like that," said Shimmer Leaf, and Addie sighed with relief. "She's hiding somewhere and none of us can find her. But Addie, maybe you can."

Addie frowned. It wasn't like Sky Dance to hide. Sky Dance was confident and strong, fearless and positive. Something very bad must have happened.

They continued toward the cluster of trees at the gateway to Wishing Wing Grove. Shimmer Leaf took off from Clara's shoulder and landed on a nearby branch.

"Okay," said the butterfly. "So this is what we know so far. This morning at the Changing Tree, another chrysalis opened. Her name's Blue Rain. When we were caterpillars, Blue Rain was always the quiet one. Very sweet and sensitive. But when she came out of her chrysalis this morning, she was definitely not quiet. Or sweet. OR sensitive!"

"Uh-oh," said Clara.

"Uh-oh is right," agreed Shimmer Leaf. "The first thing she did was fly to a branch of the Changing Tree and start shouting mean things to everyone she saw. She called one Wishing Wing a 'six-legged freak.'"

"But all butterflies have six legs!" exclaimed Addie. "Including her!"

"Exactly," said Shimmer Leaf. "She was just being grumpy and nasty for no reason. It didn't make sense, until we realized the dark enchantment must be making her act like this."

The dark enchantment seemed to work in different ways on each New Bloom. When Shimmer Leaf had emerged from her chrysalis, the enchantment had kept her from knowing who or what she was. It had made Tiger Streak think she was a bee. *Now*, thought Addie, *it must be causing Blue Rain to rain unhappiness on everyone.*

Shimmer Leaf continued filling them in. "When Sky Dance heard, she went straight to the Changing Tree to get a handle on the situation. We know she spoke to Blue Rain. Next thing anyone saw, Sky Dance was flying straight and fast out of there. One butterfly heard her crying. Nobody's seen her since."

Addie's heart crumpled to think of Sky Dance so upset. "Blue Rain must have said something that really shook her up."

"Yes, I think so too," said Shimmer Leaf. "You have to find her, Addie. And of course, we have to help Blue Rain earn her magic and break the enchantment. But first things first."

Addie nodded, then closed her eyes. She pictured Sky Dance in her head, her magic butterfly friend's beautiful pink-and-turquoise wings covered in cloud patterns.

Sky Dance! I'm here in Wishing Wing Grove to help you. Where are you?

Addie remained quiet, her eyes shut tight. She could hear crickets in the distance. The squawk of a bird high up in a tree somewhere. The *flit-flut* of butterfly wings and the soft jingle of rushing water in the nearby creek. But nothing from Sky Dance. Addie wasn't sure this was going to work. She'd never had a magical thought connection with anything before. Was it like a telephone? Was there a way to "call" her friend?

Suddenly, her head filled not with a sound but . . . a feeling. A feeling of deep, dark sadness. It was so powerful, Addie let out a sob.

"What's wrong?" asked Clara, putting her hand on her sister's shoulder.

"She's hurting," said Addie.

"Who hurt her?" growled Shimmer Leaf. "Where is she hurting? Her wing? Her legs?"

"It's not pain in her body," said Addie, shaking her head. "It's pain in her heart."

Shimmer Leaf's antennae and wings drooped. "You mean . . . her *feelings* are hurt?"

"Yes." Addie was sure of it now.

"It must have been something Blue Rain said to her," said Clara.

Shimmer Leaf rolled her big bead-like eyes. "You've got to be kidding me. She flew away and hid because of that?"

"I can find her," said Addie, but inside she was thinking, *I think I can find her. I hope I can find her.* She closed her eyes again and listened. Now she heard something:

I am not, I am not, I am not, I am not.

Addie took a few steps, and the voice grew the tiniest bit louder in her head.

Am not! She's wrong! The thoughts from Sky Dance continued, and Addie let them guide her farther into Wishing Wing Grove. She moved past the Changing Tree, which was a huge willow with branches reaching and twisting in every direction. Then along the creek, its water clear as glass, its banks dotted with yellow crickets who shared the Grove with the butterflies and made catchy music. Sky Dance's thoughts stopped being words and changed to soft cries. Addie's feet seemed to know where they were going even if she didn't.

Eventually, Addie reached a willow tree on the edge of the creek. Its roots were thick and knotted, and underneath this tangle, there was a little cave of dirt and rocks. Addie sat on the biggest root and put her head between her legs so it hung upside down, looking into the blackness of the cave. She couldn't see anything, but Sky Dance's cries were louder than ever.

"Sky Dance? Are you in there?"

All was quiet for a moment. Then Addie heard a shaky voice say, "Yes."

"Will you come out and talk to me?"

After another pause, Sky Dance said softly, "Okay."

The butterfly slowly emerged from the dark. Addie put her hand out and Sky Dance climbed onto it. Addie sat upright again, a little dizzy as the blood rushed out of her head, and held her friend carefully on her palm.

"Hi," said Addie.

"Hi," said Sky Dance. "I guess you found my secret place."

"I won't tell anyone about it," said Addie. "Why were you crying? Why did you run away?"

Sky Dance took a deep breath. "There's a New Bloom named Blue Rain . . ."

"Shimmer told us. She came out of her chrysalis and started acting not-so-nice."

"She was awful!" exclaimed Sky Dance with a little sob. "I flew over to welcome her, and do you know what she said?"

"Something mean?"

"She said, 'You think you can tell people what to do because your mother's the queen!' She told me I'm not royal, I'm just a bossy know-it-all! And that she's going to call me Princess Pig-Head from now on!" Sky Dance's wings went limp and flopped to the ground. "I am not bossy! I am not a know-it-all! Sometimes I hate being a princess!"

Addie wished she could reach out and hug Sky Dance, but she knew butterfly-hugging was not really possible. Instead, she reached out one finger and gently stroked one of Sky Dance's silky, cloud-patterned wings.

"Some people are really good at finding the one thing you feel insecure about," said Addie. "In my world, we call those people bullies."

"How do you deal with them?"

"We try to ignore them. A bully wants to see you run away and cry, so if you don't do that, you've taken away that person's power over you. If we're going to break this dark enchantment, we're going to have to ignore Blue Rain too."

"Ignore her," repeated Sky Dance. "Okay. I think I can do that."

Then they heard a voice shouting, "A HUMAN?" Startled, Addie looked up to see where it was coming from. Another

Wishing Wing perched on the trunk of the tree. The butterfly's wings were bright, brilliant purple and deep blue, covered in raindrop patterns. Addie had never before thought of rain as so lovely, but in this moment, she understood that it was.

"Hi," said Addie.

"Ew, it *talked* to me," said Blue Rain with a sneer in her voice. She sounded so much like the meanest girl at Addie's old school, it was eerie. "I hate everything about humans," said Blue Rain. "But you know what I hate most?"

Addie almost replied *What?* but caught herself.

"I hate their foreheads! Why do you have foreheads, anyway? They're huge and pointless!"

Addie opened her mouth to reply, but she was so shocked, nothing came out. She'd never told anyone, but she'd always felt self-conscious about her forehead. She thought maybe it was too wide for her face.

Blue Rain laughed loud and long into the silence, then flew off.

CHAPTER THREE

Addie stared at the space where Blue Rain had been, feeling like she'd just been stung. She'd had this feeling before, whenever another kid said something mean to her and she didn't know how to respond. But she'd never expected to get this feeling from a butterfly!

"I know," said Sky Dance, flying to land on Addie's shoulder. "She's so mean."

"It's obviously the dark enchantment making her act this way, but still . . . that really hurt."

Sky Dance tilted her head sideways, thinking a bit. "This enchantment will be a tough one to break. But break it we must!" The Wishing Wing's eyes suddenly grew wide. "That's not being bossy, is it?"

"No," said Addie, laughing. "That's just being determined. Let's find our butterfly sisters and figure out how to help Blue Rain."

Suddenly, Addie heard Clara calling for her.

"We're over here!" Addie shouted back, drawing aside the hanging branches of the willow tree to see her sister and Shimmer Leaf.

"Sky!" exclaimed Shimmer, and the

butterfly sisters rushed together, flitting in joyful circles around each other. *I guess that's how you hug when you have wings instead of arms*, thought Addie.

"I'm okay," said Sky Dance. "Blue Rain was aiming to hurt me, and she did at first. But now I'm not going to let her."

"Good," said Clara. "We need to get her to the human world so someone can catch and release her and break the spell."

"That won't be easy," said Addie. "Blue Rain says she hates humans."

"Mama will know what to do," said Shimmer Leaf.

They all agreed that finding the butterflies' mother, Queen Rose Glow, was a good first step. Sky Dance led the way toward the giant boulder where the Queen, along with her husband King Flit Flash, would be holding court.

As they came upon a small hill covered with pebbles, a high voice greeted them.

"Well, hello!" chirped the voice.

Surprised, Addie turned to see a long, thin, neon-green caterpillar perched on the largest pebble. It was Queen Rose Glow's friend Madame Furia. Despite her slightly creepy appearance—she had red spikes all the way down her back—she always seemed wise and cheerful.

"Hi, Madame Furia," said Sky Dance, hovering above the caterpillar.

"What are you girls up to?" asked Madame Furia, one red eye pointing at Addie, the other pointing at Clara.

"We're on our way to talk to Mama," said Shimmer Leaf. "Blue Rain emerged this morning. The dark enchantment has made her—"

"A rather unpleasant Wishing Wing?"

Furia cut in. "I know. She came by this way and said some absolutely dreadful things about my spikes. I like my spikes! They're good for hanging things on!"

Furia smiled and winked one of her red eyes at them. Addie was about to say *Nice to see you, but we're in a rush*, when Furia took a deep sigh and kept talking.

"Of course, I hated them at first," said Furia. "They started growing right after your grandmother Queen Silver Star cast the enchantment that would keep me from becoming a butterfly."

Addie knew that Madame Furia had once been like every other caterpillar in Wishing Wing Grove—one who would, at the right time, spin a chrysalis at the

Changing Tree and emerge as a New Bloom, ready to grant a wish from a human child and earn her Wishing Wing magic. But Furia had broken the rules of the caterpillar nursery and was given a punishment: she would stay a caterpillar forever.

"I think your spikes are cool," said Clara. "Anyway, we'd love to stay and talk, but we really must be going . . ."

"Did you know my name used to be Golden Burst?" asked Madame Furia, as if she hadn't heard Clara.

Sky Dance and Shimmer Leaf landed on pebbles next to Furia. Addie saw their antennae straighten up and curl in curiosity toward the caterpillar.

"That's pretty!" said Sky Dance. "Why are you called Madame Furia now?"

"Well," said Furia, "since I couldn't

change into a butterfly, I wanted to change *somehow*. So I changed my name! I had trouble managing my temper back then . . . and the name "Furia" felt like it fit me. After all, it was my temper that got me into trouble in the first place."

"Addie," whispered Clara, tugging on Addie's shirt. "We don't have time for this."

"Yeah, but aren't you curious?" Addie whispered back. "Plus, she seems really lonely and needs someone to talk to."

Clearly Sky Dance and Shimmer Leaf were eager to listen to Furia's side of a story they'd heard their whole lives. "Mama said you two were best friends," said Sky Dance to Furia.

"We were," replied Furia with a smile. "Inseparable, in fact! But your mother was always very friendly and started spending time with another caterpillar too. I got jealous. I thought this caterpillar was trying to steal your mother away from me, and I'd be left with no friends. But instead of talking to Rose Glow about it, I did the wrong thing."

"Mama said you stole food from the nursery and made it look like the other caterpillar did it."

"Shimmer, hush!" scolded Sky Dance. "Don't be disrespectful."

"It's okay," said Furia. "She's right. That's exactly what I did. I was young, and it was a mistake. I'm happy with who I am now, although I wasn't at first. I was so angry about the punishment, I left Wishing Wing Grove."

"Where did you go?" asked Clara. Now she was sucked in too.

"Oh, I visited Wasp Point, Bee Hollow,

Ant Mountain . . . It was fascinating to see what life was like in other kingdoms!"

"Wow!" said Sky Dance. "Someday you'll have to tell us more."

"Someday?" asked Madame Furia. "Why not now?"

"We have to figure out a way to bring Blue Rain to the human world so we can help her grant a wish."

"Oh, right!" laughed Furia. "I forgot you were in a hurry. I'm so sorry. Thank you for keeping a lonely caterpillar company for a little while."

"Anytime," said Sky Dance, flying ahead to lead the way for Addie, Clara, and Shimmer Leaf. "We'll come by again soon to hear more!"

As they left Madame Furia's hill, Addie looked back to see the caterpillar smiling at them. It was nice that they'd stopped to talk to her.

After a few minutes, the two pairs of sisters came upon the large boulder where Queen Rose Glow held court. The boulder looked like the inside of a kaleidoscope, covered with the dazzling, moving colors and patterns of dozens of Wishing Wings.

Sky Dance and Shimmer Leaf flew on ahead, landing at the top of the boulder between their parents. As Addie and Clara approached, Addie heard many Wishing Wing voices talking over one another.

"She called me Shrimpy Wings!" sniffled one. "I can't help it that my wings are on the small side!"

"She said I don't know how to fly

straight," shouted another. "I fly crooked on purpose! It's more fun that way!"

Addie and Clara found a spot near the boulder and stood by quietly to watch what happened next.

"She doesn't act the way a Wishing Wing should act!" said one butterfly. "I say, let her lose her magic, and then banish her!"

There were cheers of "Yes!" and "Good idea!" coming from the other butterflies, until a loud clapping sound shook the air around them. Then another. Queen Rose Glow was banging her wings together. The red rose patterns on them lit up and sparkled in the sunlight. That got everyone's attention.

"Enough!" commanded Rose Glow. "Don't you remember? Every time a New Bloom fails to earn its magic, it weakens the magic of all Wishing Wings! I believe this is the ultimate goal of the dark enchantment. Thankfully, with the help of our human friends Addie and Clara, we have thwarted the enchantment twice. We will do it again for Blue Rain."

A murmur rose up among the gathered butterflies.

"I know it's hard," continued Rose Glow, "but you must remember, Blue Rain's behavior is not her fault. It is not the real Blue Rain acting this way. It's the enchantment. We will stand together and help her, because she's as much a Wishing Wing as every one of us."

"The Queen is right!" called Sky Dance.

King Flit Flash turned to Addie and Clara. "Do you agree, dear friends?"

Addie thought for a moment. What

Queen Rose Glow said made sense. She stepped forward.

"Yes!" said Addie. "Clara and I will do whatever we can to help Blue Rain grant her first wish."

"But how?" asked the butterfly who Blue Rain had called "Shrimpy Wings."

Queen Rose Glow's words echoed in Addie's head. *It is not the real Blue Rain acting this way.*

Then, Morgan's words from earlier: *It all started when Oliver's big brother left for the Navy.*

It suddenly became crystal clear to Addie. Oliver was also under a type of dark enchantment—an enchantment otherwise known as "sadness."

"Clara!" she exclaimed. "We've got to get Blue Rain together with that boy Oliver! He's the perfect person to catch her!"

Clara wrinkled up her nose. "Ew. Really?"

"Absolutely!" said Addie. Then she addressed the butterflies. "Clara and I have a plan. Can we count on all of you to help if we need it?"

Another murmur rose up among the butterflies.

"I will help!" shouted Sky Dance.

"Me too! Whatever you need!" added Shimmer Leaf.

"You shall have anything you need from me," chimed in Queen Rose Glow.

"And me, of course," said King Flit Flash.

Then Addie heard other butterflies piping up—"Yes!" "Me too!" "I'm in!"— and knew that once again, the Wishing Wings were united, as they should be.

"Excellent!" said Addie. "So now we need to rush home and talk to Oliver."

"Let us make your trip shorter," said Rose Glow, and she broke into a mischievous, magical smile.

Addie knew what that meant, and her heart jumped with excitement.

CHAPTER FOUR

Rose Glow and Flit Flash winked at each other. Sky Dance and Shimmer Leaf both laughed.

The Wishing Wing royal family was about to make some very special magic.

Addie took a few steps away from Clara. Then she stood very still as Rose Glow and Sky Dance zipped into the air together, touching their wings. They began to fly a circle around Addie, trailing a sparkling rainbow of their colors behind them. Red, green, silver, turquoise, pink, white. Addie closed her eyes and for the first time could *feel* the magic dancing around her. It almost tickled.

She peeped with one eye to glimpse Flit Flash and Shimmer Leaf. They were flying around Clara in the same way, their wings touching. Addie knew each

butterfly pair would fly around them three times. She wondered if she'd know when they were done.

And she did. In one amazing moment, she felt light and free. She could feel the breeze on her arms. No. Not arms. WINGS!

Addie opened her eyes and saw that she was small now, butterfly-size. Her wings always came out of the magic

looking the same: magenta and powder blue, with lavender hearts on them. *This must be what my butterfly spirit looks like,* she thought.

Clara laughed. She also had the same wings as before: deep pink and orange, with flames on them.

"No time to admire yourselves!" said Rose Glow. "Hurry home!"

Addie knew the magic would wear off in a few minutes. If they flew quickly, they could make it.

"Come on!" she shouted, turning to Clara. But Clara had already taken wing, so then Addie had to yell, "Wait for me!" and rocket herself into the air.

"They're no slowpokes!" laughed Shimmer Leaf as she whooshed off behind them. Sky Dance followed.

The two pairs of sisters flew out of

Wishing Wing Grove and over the dancing grass of Silk Meadow. Into the woods, past trees that Addie recognized even though they were much bigger now. Or rather, she was much smaller. She looked down and saw her own footprints from before. How strange that she didn't have those feet at the moment! She felt light and fast and fearless.

In no time at all, the butterflies were zooming past the trees behind Addie's house. Whoa! Their backyard looked huge from here! And their house looked like a mansion. One a giant might live in. Addie giggled at how weird and wonderful it all was.

"Hey," said Clara, flying close to Addie. "Let's keep going. We can take a tour of the neighborhood while we're up here!"

"Definitely!" shouted Addie. Now she

took the lead; she wasn't going to let Clara be in charge the whole time. They sped past their house—it looked even bigger from the front!—and toward the road. They followed the road in a direction they'd never been, past one, two, then three houses. Addie saw an elderly neighbor walking two huge dogs, a baby playing in a kiddie pool with his mother nearby, and a chalk drawing of a monster on a driveway.

"We should probably head back to your yard," warned Sky Dance, flying close to her. "Make sure you land where no humans can see you."

Addie nodded. She circled around the third house and into that backyard, over the head of a man mowing his lawn. In the next backyard, a woman was sitting in a chair, working on her computer.

This is like spying, said Addie to herself.

When she reached the next backyard, Addie saw sparkles flashing in her eyes. She felt herself flying slower, and her body seemed heavier. She knew the magic was wearing off and headed for the ground, hoping she could pull off a soft landing. Fortunately, there was nobody in this yard.

A gentle *thud*, and then suddenly she was rolling in grass.

"Ow!" she heard Clara shout.

"Clara, you're going to have to work on recognizing when it's time to land!" said Shimmer Leaf. She and Sky Dance had come to rest on a nearby rock. "Are you okay?"

"I will be in a minute," replied Clara as she took a deep breath. "Where are we?"

"One of the neighbors' backyards, I guess," said Addie, sitting up and wiping grass off her face. She looked around and saw their own house through some trees. "Oh! We're right next door to home!"

"Right next door?" repeated Clara slowly.

"Yup!"

"But that means . . . this must be Oliver's house." Clara's voice was full of dread.

"Holy moly, you're right," said Addie. "It'll be super awkward if he sees us here. Let's go around and knock on the front door."

"I'll catch up in a minute," said Sky Dance. "When we were flying, I got some pollen on myself and it's driving me crazy." She began cleaning her left antenna with her two front legs.

Addie and Clara crouched low, as if they were pretending to be cats, and ran as quickly and quietly as they could toward the side of the house. Shimmer Leaf fluttered along next to them.

"Not. So. Fast."

The girls froze and slowly turned around.

Oliver was standing before them, his hands on his hips. It was like he'd dropped out of the sky (and she'd thought they were the only ones who could do that!). Addie glanced up and saw a treehouse above their heads. Okay, so maybe he *had* dropped out of the sky . . . sort of.

Addie gulped, then cleared her throat.

She wasn't good at meeting new people, especially in weird situations like this.

"Hi!" said Clara extra-cheerfully before Addie could open her mouth. Clara was much better under pressure. "You must be Oliver!"

"And you must be the new girls," he said, not sounding the least bit friendly or excited about it.

"Yes, we live—"

"Right next door," said Oliver, rolling his eyes. "Duh. I know. What I don't know is, why are you in *my* backyard?"

Addie finally found her voice. "We were just . . ." she began, not sure how to finish the statement.

"You're here to prank me, aren't you? To get even for that thing with the doorbell."

"No, we're not!" said Addie.

"Give me a break. Of course you are. I'm sure Morgan told you all about me."

"She did!" said Clara, stepping toward Oliver and standing just like him, with her hands on her hips. She looked confident and brave. "She told us you used to be nice, and that the two of you were friends. And now you go around pranking everyone and have no friends anymore. We can see why! We just came over here to say hi, and look how you're treating us!"

Oliver looked at them, his lip trembling.

Addie felt glad Clara had stood up to him, but also a little sad for him, too.

"Shut up!" exclaimed Oliver. "Go away!" He sniffled, then ran around the corner of his house.

They all paused for a few moments, not sure what to do next. Addie hoped Oliver would change his mind and come back.

"Come on," said Clara finally, tugging on Addie's sleeve. "Let's go home and brainstorm."

Shimmer Leaf landed on Clara's shoulder and said, "You're right. He does need a wish. The trick will be getting him to catch Blue Rain. Are you coming, Sky Dance?"

But Sky Dance didn't answer.

Addie looked over to the rock where

Sky Dance had been just a few seconds ago, but the butterfly was gone.

There was only Oliver standing next to it.

With a butterfly net.

And Sky Dance trapped inside.

CHAPTER FIVE

N o!" squealed Shimmer Leaf.

"Let her go!" shouted Addie.

Clara didn't say anything. She just raced toward Oliver.

Oliver was too fast for her, though. Holding the net closed with one of his hands, he started scrambling up to his treehouse. The treehouse had a trap-door entrance. As soon as Oliver climbed through it, the door slammed shut. Clara climbed up the ladder, pounding on the door from below.

After a minute, Oliver appeared in the treehouse's single window. He held up a large jar. Inside, Sky Dance fluttered frantically. Addie could see her banging her wings against the glass.

"This is the coolest butterfly I've ever seen!" called Oliver. "And now it's mine!"

He disappeared from the window. Clara gave up and climbed down from the tree, trying to catch her breath. "Okay, so our plan just got a lot more complicated. Let's get out of here and brainstorm."

As Addie led the way back to their

own yard, Shimmer Leaf paused in the air a few times to look back at Oliver's treehouse, her eyes wide with worry. Clara showed them the secret spot she'd found under the deck during their hide-and-seek game. It was barely tall and wide enough for both girls to sit. Addie crawled in after Clara and noticed how soft and cool the dirt felt. *A little gross,* thought Addie, *but also pretty neat.* Shimmer Leaf flitted back and forth between them, up and down in little figure eights. Her wings quivered.

"Whatever we do, we have to do it quickly!" cried the Wishing Wing.

"Can't Sky Dance use her magic to get out of the jar?" asked Clara.

"No," replied Shimmer Leaf, shaking her head. "She needs to be able to fly around something three times to turn it into something else. If the jar's empty, she has nothing to work with."

"Then we should go storm the tree-house!" said Clara.

Addie knew in her heart that wouldn't work. *Storming a treehouse* sounded like something that would get parents involved, and any adult who saw Sky Dance would know she was no ordinary butterfly. No, they couldn't be stormy . . . they had to be *stealthy*.

"We'll sneak in," said Addie.

Clara's angry expression turned thoughtful. "You mean, wait until Oliver's not there?"

"Or lure him out with some kind of distraction," Addie suggested.

Addie was thinking as she was talking.

A picture was forming in her head. What could possibly bring Oliver out of his treehouse after catching the most unusual butterfly he'd ever seen?

Well, that was simple: *Another* unusual butterfly.

Suddenly, the whole plan was clear and complete in Addie's head, like a finished puzzle.

"My sister!" sobbed Shimmer Leaf. "She must be so frightened!"

Addie closed her eyes and listened for Sky Dance's thoughts.

But she heard only silence, and then Shimmer Leaf's shaky voice. "You won't hear her," said the butterfly. "Butterfly magic won't travel through glass."

Addie reached out her palm to the panicked Wishing Wing, and Shimmer Leaf landed on it.

"It's going to be okay," said Addie. "I think I have a plan."

She told Clara and Shimmer Leaf about her idea.

"Blue Rain hates humans, right? Shimmer, you go back to the Grove and tell Blue Rain that a human has captured Sky Dance. Say we need her help because she's tough and strong and speaks her mind. I'll bet she loves being flattered like that. Lead her back to Oliver's yard, and I'll make sure Oliver sees her. While he and I are busy trying to catch Blue Rain, Clara, you sneak into the treehouse and free Sky Dance."

Addie took a deep breath. Her plan sounded just as good out loud as it had in her head.

"That's all possible," said Clara, "except for the part where Oliver will have to set Blue Rain *free* in order to break the enchantment. I don't exactly see him doing that."

"True," agreed Addie. "We'll have to figure that part out later. But at least we have something to start with. Are you guys in?"

"I'm in," Clara said, and high-fived her sister.

Shimmer was silent for a moment, then she zoomed from Addie's palm into the air.

"I'm in too," Shimmer said. The girls still had their hands up, and Shimmer Leaf fluttered against each of them. "We Wishing Wings call that a 'high-fly!'"

Clara giggled, and Addie couldn't help giggling too. She felt a little better now. Maybe everything would work out.

A sudden, loud bark interrupted their laughter.

Addie and Clara crawled out of their hiding spot just in time to see their dog, Pepper, chasing their new kitten, Squish, across the deck and into the yard. The orange kitten bounded up a nearby tree. Then she climbed up even more.

Two days ago, Squish had been a raggedy orange-and-white stuffed animal. Now, thanks to Shimmer Leaf granting Clara's wish for a pet, Squish was a real live kitten that Pepper was, er, having a bit of trouble getting used to.

"Squish!" yelled Clara, running toward the tree, where Pepper was now yipping and running in circles.

Addie quickly followed. When she reached Pepper, she scooped him up in her arms and brought him back to the house. Someone had left the back door slightly open. "Stop making trouble," she scolded the dog as she pushed him inside and slid the door shut.

When Addie turned back to the yard, she saw Clara pulling herself up onto the lowest branch of the tree. Squish was huddled two branches up.

"It's safe now, Squishy!" she called to the blob of orange fur barely visible among the pine needles. "I'll help you get back down!"

Clara grabbed the next branch with one hand and stretched her other arm toward the kitten. But Squish didn't budge. Clara reached higher, her fingertips brushing his side. Addie held her breath. For one second, it looked like Clara was about to grab Squish, and then

the next second, she was sprawled on the ground.

"Ow!' Clara cried.

Addie rushed to her sister. Shimmer Leaf darted toward her too, landing on Clara's chest.

"Are you okay?" asked Addie.

Clara sat up and grabbed her left foot. "My ankle hurts. I think I twisted it when I landed."

Addie turned to Shimmer Leaf, who was still clinging to Clara's shirt. "Can you fix it?"

Shimmer Leaf tapped two of her right legs against the side of her head. "I can definitely help," she said after a few moments of thinking. "But it won't be instant. Do you have something you can wrap around her ankle?"

Addie considered this, then reached

up and touched the ribbon she'd tied around her ponytail that morning. It was Addie's favorite ribbon: pink with black hearts on it. She'd bought it with birthday money at a craft fair. But Clara was hurt.

"Here," said Addie as she pulled the ribbon loose quickly, before she could change her mind. She looped it several times around Clara's ankle, which was already looking swollen, then tied it into a bow.

"Lift her foot as high as you can," said Shimmer Leaf, and Addie did just that.

Shimmer Leaf whooshed into the air and flew the first circle around Clara's ankle, leaving a trail of purple, peach, and mint green behind her as she went. *Maybe I can find a new ribbon, in Shimmer Leaf's colors*, thought Addie as she watched. Shimmer Leaf flew another circle, then a third, until the stripes began flashing and popping like sparklers. When they vanished, Addie saw the result.

Clara's ankle was now wrapped in a thick, soft bandage that was pink with black hearts on it.

"It's got healing magic," said Shimmer Leaf. "But the magic will take a while to work because I'm still a newbie at this stuff. You can't move yet. I'm going to fly on ahead to find Blue Rain. I'll bring her back and meet you in Oliver's yard."

Shimmer Leaf jetted away into the woods. Addie heard a frightened *mew* and both girls looked up at the spot of orange in the tree.

"Poor Squish!" said Clara. "Addie, you need to get him!"

"Me?" asked Addie. "But I've never climbed a tree before. I don't know how!"

"You have to try! It's not that hard."

"How can you say that? You just fell and got hurt!"

Clara gave her a very angry look, then turned away.

She's right, though, thought Addie. *I should at least try.*

If they left Squish in the tree, he might climb higher and higher. They had to get him so they could focus on Sky Dance. She was alone and scared in a glass jar, and they had no idea what Oliver planned to do with her.

Addie stood up, took a deep breath, and jumped for the first branch. But she didn't jump quite high enough, and only brushed it with her outstretched fingertips.

"Hey," said a high, cheerful voice behind her. "It looks like you could use a hand."

Addie turned, and she'd never in her life been so happy to see a bee hovering in front of her face.

"Kirby!" she exclaimed. "We're trying to get our kitten down from that branch, then we've got to help Sky Dance, who's been captured by the boy next door, and there's a New Bloom named Blue Rain and . . . well, it's a long story. We'll fill you in later."

Kirby flew up the tree to get a better look at Squish, then came down to Addie's eye level again. "Normally, I'm not a fan of felines. But they are hopelessly predictable. I know what to do here."

Kirby buzzed straight into Squish's face, bopping the kitten on the nose, then flying just out of reach. Squish stood up.

Kirby landed on the next branch down and started walking in circles.

"Look at me!" he called. "La-de-dah, I'm just a clueless bug. I'd be so easy to catch!"

Without taking his eyes off Kirby, Squish jumped down to the branch.

"Kirby's doing it!" whispered Clara. "He's luring Squish out of the tree!"

Squish reached out his paw to bat at Kirby, but Kirby shot into the air again and flew down to the next branch. They watched the same thing happen. Finally, Kirby flew down to the ground, buzzing and circling and making himself irresistible to a playful kitten.

When Squish came low enough on the tree trunk, Addie grabbed him and put him in Clara's arms.

"You poor thing!" said Clara, rubbing

her face in his fur. Addie could hear his little motorboat purr start up. "Thank you, Kirby!"

Suddenly, Addie heard something else.

Addie, are you there? Addie, please help me!

CHAPTER SIX

Sky Dance! Yes, I can hear you!
Addie stood completely still, as if moving even an inch would break their thought connection.

Shimmer said you wouldn't be able to send messages through the glass, she added.

Addie waited for a reply. The breeze picked up a bit.

It wasn't easy, answered Sky Dance. *I had to calm myself down and use every ounce of magic I've got.*

Stay calm, Addie told her with her thoughts. *We have a plan. We're coming to rescue you AND save Blue Rain.*

Hurry! said Sky Dance. *Oliver said something about showing me to his parents as soon as they came home.*

Suddenly, Clara stood up.

"Hey!" she exclaimed. "My ankle doesn't hurt anymore."

"Awesome!" said Addie. "Do you want me to unwrap it for you?"

"Take off a magical bandage? Are you nuts? I'm keeping this thing on as long as I can."

Addie laughed and shook her head. "Fine. Put Squish in the house and make sure the door is shut tight this time!"

Clara did just that, and when she came back to the tree, her face was glowing with excitement.

"Shimmer Leaf just sent me a message! Our plan is working so far: Blue Rain's on her way to distract Oliver. She loves the idea of teasing him."

"They're expecting me back at the hive," said Kirby, who'd landed on a nearby flower. "I won't go anywhere near that boy. He once tried to catch me to use in a prank!"

"You've already helped a lot," said Clara.

"Thanks again, Kirby," said Addie, then she turned to Clara. "Let's go!" she urged, and they rushed toward Oliver's house.

"What'll we say to him?" Clara asked on the way.

"Follow my lead," Addie replied.

They stepped into Oliver's yard and Addie took a spot directly under the tree-house window.

"Hey, Oliver!" she called.

There was silence for a few moments. Then Oliver's head appeared in the window. He crossed his arms over his chest.

"Oh, it's you. What do you want?"

"We just saw another butterfly come through our yard. This one was even bigger and cooler than the one you caught!"

"Ha!" said Oliver. "I doubt that!"

"Seriously," said Addie. "It was bright blue and purple and *huge!* Did you see it?"

"You're making that up. You're trying to trick me, and it won't work."

Clara stepped up beside Addie. "Fine,

don't believe us. We'll just catch the butterfly first!"

"Go away!" Oliver shouted. He slammed the window of his treehouse shut.

Addie turned to Clara. "What do we do now?"

Clara shrugged. Addie closed her eyes and sent a message to Sky Dance. *Hang in there. We'll figure something out.*

As soon as she thought those words, she heard fluttering behind her. She felt the tip of something graze the top of her hair. Addie looked up . . .

It was Blue Rain!

The Wishing Wing rocketed over their heads, moving faster than Addie'd ever seen one fly. That wasn't normal butterfly flying. That was *angry* flying.

Addie heard another flutter and turned

to see Shimmer Leaf landing on Clara's shoulder.

"Mission accomplished," Shimmer Leaf whispered.

"Clearly," said Addie, watching Blue Rain fly in furious circles around Oliver's backyard.

"Where is he?" shouted Blue Rain. "The human who catches butterflies and puts them in jars?"

Addie pointed at the treehouse and Blue Rain started circling it immediately. *Good thing she doesn't have magic yet,* thought Addie. *Who knows what she'd try to do!*

"Oliver!" Clara yelled up to the closed window. "The butterfly's right here! Come look!"

The window swung open and Oliver's face appeared again, this time with a big scowl on it. But then he spotted Blue Rain jetting past at eye level. His mouth dropped open in amazement. Two seconds later, he was scrambling down the tree, his butterfly net in one hand and another jar in the other.

"I'm going to catch this one first," he teased Addie and Clara. "You two don't even have a net!"

Blue Rain kept flying angrily around the yard. Oliver began chasing her with the net.

"Now's our chance!" whispered Clara. "I'm going to climb up and get Sky Dance!"

"You?" asked Addie.

"Yes, me. You're afraid of heights, remember?"

Addie remembered. It made her cringe, to think about how frightened she'd been.

Clara took a step toward the tree, but Addie found herself reaching out and grabbing her sister's arm.

"Wait. I'll do it. Your ankle may still be healing."

And I'm embarrassed to have this particular fear, she added to herself.

Don't be embarrassed, she heard Sky Dance say. *But it's always good to face your fears. Especially if it means getting me out of this jar!*

Addie smiled to herself, then took a

deep breath. She reached out her arms and grabbed the first branch, putting her foot on the lowest wooden block nailed to the trunk.

Clara ran over to Oliver and pretended to help him. "Look, it's over there!" she called as Blue Rain flew another wide circle around them.

Addie hoisted her body up, first an arm, then a foot. Again, and then again. She was determined not to look down, and determined not to think about how much it would hurt to fall and land on the ground below.

"It went thataway!" Addie heard Oliver shout, and saw him beginning to run toward the treehouse. She had to hurry if she didn't want to be spotted.

One more branch and one more

foothold, and she would be able to open the trapdoor. Addie reached . . . and stepped . . .

She was there! She put her palm on the wooden door and pushed it up. She pulled herself into the treehouse and closed the door just as Oliver was running past the tree.

Addie spotted the jar in a corner of the treehouse. What she saw inside almost broke her heart.

Sky Dance was huddled against the glass, her wings folded around her like a blanket. Her antennae drooped, and her eyes were shut tight.

Addie grabbed the jar and held it up to her face.

"Sky Dance! It's me! I'm here!"

Sky Dance opened her eyes slowly. They lit up as soon as she saw Addie.

Addie wasted no time. She unscrewed the lid and Sky Dance shot out of the jar, leaving a trail of pink and turquoise behind her.

"Oops, sorry," said Sky Dance as she circled back and landed on Addie's shoulder. "I do that when I'm excited."

Addie glanced around the treehouse. There was nothing here except a small rug in the corner with some pillows. Next to it sat a pile of books, a stationery set, and a few empty peanut butter jars, scraped clean. On one wall, Oliver had posted several photographs of himself and a much older boy, smiling for the camera. That must be his big brother.

Oliver was sad, for sure, and the treehouse was a place to be alone with his sadness (and to eat peanut butter, apparently!). It really was like Blue Rain's

enchantment, because the way he acted outside of the treehouse . . . well, that wasn't him.

Despite the fact that Oliver had been nothing but grumpy to Addie so far, she really wanted him to have a wish come true. He really needed one.

"Let's go see if we can help Oliver catch Blue Rain," said Addie as she opened the trapdoor again. Sky Dance flew out, then circled back.

"The coast is clear!" said Sky Dance. "But make it quick!"

It looked even more difficult to climb *down* from a tree than it had been to climb up, but Addie knew this was no time to let fear get the best of her. She went as quickly, and as safely, as she could. Before she knew it, her left foot was touching solid ground.

"Here they come," whispered Sky Dance. "I'm going to make myself scarce."

The butterfly tucked herself into the V between two tree branches just as Oliver, Clara, and Blue Rain rounded the corner from the front of her house.

Blue Rain must have seen Sky Dance, because she came to land on the branch above Sky Dance's hiding place.

"So, you're free now! With my help, of course!"

"Yes," whispered Sky Dance. "Thank you."

"I guess even bossy princesses can be careless. Hopefully you've learned your lesson."

Sky Dance blinked hard a few times, and Addie could tell her friend was trying not to let Blue Rain get to her. Then the butterfly spotted something over

Addie's shoulder and her eyes grew wide. She ducked behind a branch.

"Remember that time you came to visit the Caterpillar Nursery?" continued Blue Rain in her mean voice. "You told me to eat—"

Swish.

The net came down quickly and hard over Blue Rain.

"Got it!" yelped Oliver.

Clara came running up behind him, breathless. When she saw that Oliver had finally caught Blue Rain, she smiled. Then she looked at Addie and silently mouthed the words "Sky Dance?" Addie nodded yes. Clara pumped her fist.

"Set it free, Oliver," said Addie.

"Why should I? Now I have *two* rare butterflies, and everyone's going to want to see them!"

"Oliver, please," urged Clara. "Something wonderful will happen if you just set the butterfly free, I promise."

Oliver frowned. "You can't prank me. I'm the king of pranks."

"We're not pranking," begged Addie. "We swear!"

"No!" he said.

He shook Blue Rain from the net into the jar and slammed the lid on tight.

CHAPTER SEVEN

O liver sat down on the ground and hugged the jar to his chest.

For the first time that day, Addie began to worry that maybe their plan wouldn't work. She took a deep breath. No. She would not give up! Not yet.

"Oliver," she pleaded. "Why do you need to keep this butterfly?"

"Because," said Oliver, his expression turning sad. "I just do."

"That's not a good enough reason!" Clara insisted. "You can't just catch living things and make them yours. Admire them for a few minutes, sure, but not forever."

Oliver was quiet. Addie hoped Clara's words were getting through to him.

Finally, Oliver swallowed hard and said, "I need something to keep me company. I need a . . ." Then Oliver stopped himself, biting his lip. Addie saw the beginnings of tears in his eyes.

"Friend?" she asked softly.

Oliver didn't answer, but he didn't need to. The way he hunched his shoulders and stared at the ground said it all.

"You and Morgan could be friends again," suggested Addie.

"And if you let this butterfly go, we'll be your friends, too," added Clara.

Oliver looked up at them, but then shook his head. "Everybody hates me now. I'm sure you guys do, too."

Blue Rain had finally stopped fluttering inside the jar. Now she was huddled against the glass, her wings drooping. She must have been too tired and dejected to shout insults anymore.

Addie turned to Clara and leaned in close to her sister's ear.

"What do we do now?"

"I don't know," whispered Clara, her voice drained of confidence. "I'm out of ideas."

Addie glanced at the sky to see the sun resting above the treetops. It wouldn't be long before it started setting. They were running short on time.

Whoosh. Whoosh.

It was a strange sound above them. A low-flying bird? Addie looked around, but saw nothing.

Whoosh. Whoosh.

Clara heard it, too. Both girls spun slowly in a circle, trying to locate the source of the noise.

Whoosh. Whoosh. Whoosh. Whoosh.

Louder and faster now! Oliver jumped up; clearly, he'd heard it as well.

"What was that?" he shouted.

"There!" called Clara, pointing excitedly.

Rising out of the woods was the biggest, most brilliant butterfly Addie had ever seen. It was the size of Oliver's treehouse! She was a bit frightened . . . but also amazed . . . and definitely confused. Was this a Wishing Wing?

Oliver's mouth had dropped into a big O. He just whispered, "Whoa," which really did seem like the most appropriate thing to say.

The butterfly drew closer, and suddenly Addie understood.

Clara did, too. "Oh my goodness," she said breathlessly. "It's *all* of them."

This wasn't one enormous butterfly. This was hundreds of Wishing Wings, flying together! In the shape of one giant butterfly! Queen Rose Glow and King Flit Flash were at the top, acting as the butterfly's "head." The wings were a mosaic of every color and pattern Addie could imagine.

Rose Glow must have sensed through her magic that some extra-special help was called for, and all the Wishing Wings had come together to make it happen.

The formation hovered in the air right above Oliver, flapping its wings slowly.

Addie knew what to do next.

"See, Oliver," she said. "This butterfly has a family. She would miss them terribly if you kept her. You know what it's like to miss someone, right?"

Oliver looked at Addie. At first, he seemed embarrassed, but then tears came back to his eyes. He simply bit his lip and nodded.

He reached for the lid of the jar. Addie held her breath and exchanged a hopeful look with Clara. The enormous mass of Wishing Wing butterflies continued to flap its wings.

Oliver lifted the lid.

At first, Blue Rain didn't even seem to notice. She stayed curled up, her eyes closed.

Did that count as setting her free? Addie wondered.

Blue Rain's big, dark eyes popped open now. Her little head snapped up. Her wings straightened out and the colors on them went from dimmed to glowing again.

"Yee-haw!" she squealed, darting straight up into the air. She flew a giant figure eight above them, then circled the giant butterfly formation. The shape fell apart as all the Wishing Wings surrounded Blue Rain. Addie spotted Tiger Streak, with her yellow, orange, and black tiger-stripes, flitting among them. Sky Dance and Shimmer Leaf burst out of their hiding place and flew to join their parents. It was the happiest and most beautiful reunion Addie had ever seen. Eventually, all the Wishing Wings settled onto the branches surrounding the treehouse. It reminded Addie of a Christmas tree covered in colorful ornaments.

"Whoa," Oliver said again, and sank back down to the ground.

Blue Rain paused in mid-air when she heard his voice, then fluttered her way back toward him. She landed on his knee and said, "Hi."

Oliver was quiet. "Double whoa," he finally said.

"I'm Blue Rain. You caught me and set me free, didn't you?"

Oliver nodded, his eyes wide.

"That means I owe you a wish! You have nice eyes, by the way. They're so brown!"

Oliver looked at Addie and Clara. "If this is a prank, it's the best one ever."

"Not a prank," said Clara. "Magic."

"N-n-no such thing," said Oliver,

shaking his head as if he was trying to wake himself up from a dream.

"I hope you'll feel differently after I grant you a wish," said Blue Rain shyly. She sounded so kind and sensitive now that she was no longer under the enchantment. This was the real Blue Rain!

"It's for real," said Addie. "You get just one, so choose carefully." Then she glanced at the sun resting a little lower in the trees. "But choose sort of quickly, too."

"Well, that's easy," Oliver said. "If wishes-come-true were actually a thing, I would wish for my brother to be here. With me. If you can make that happen, then I'll believe in magic butterflies."

Blue Rain tilted her head, deep in thought. She looked over at Sky Dance and Shimmer Leaf, who had landed nearby.

"I'm a wish newbie," Blue Rain said to them, a little embarrassed. "Any suggestions?"

Sky Dance paused, then Addie got a thought message from her.

The photos! In the treehouse!

Addie smiled. "Hang on," she told Oliver and Blue Rain.

She climbed the tree in a matter of seconds. She didn't have to think about where to put each hand and foot, or even to be nervous. It wasn't until she reached the trapdoor that she realized what she'd done. *Hey! Not scared of tree-climbing anymore!*

Addie removed one of Oliver's photos from the treehouse wall and tucked it carefully into her back pocket. She climbed down to the ground again.

"Here," she said, handing the photo to Oliver.

"How'd you know that was in there?" he asked with a frown.

"Never mind that," replied Addie. "Just hold it still."

Oliver gave her a doubtful look, but did as she instructed. Blue Rain took to the air and flew one slow circle around the photo. The trail she left behind was blue, purple, and white, so pretty that Addie wished she could reach out and touch it.

Oliver's jaw dropped as Blue Rain flew her second circle around the photo . . . and then a third.

Her colors started flashing and sparkling, and they all watched as the stripes slowly disappeared.

The photo had disappeared along with them.

"What happened?" asked Oliver, looking around for the photo that was no longer in his hand.

"Wait for it," said Addie. She hoped they wouldn't have to wait too long.

"Oliver!" called a voice. A woman who must be Oliver's mom opened their back door. "Your brother's on the phone!"

Oliver was up and run-ning toward the

house so quickly, it looked like a fast-motion movie. Blue Rain laughed.

"That was fun!" she said. "But wait, why are all the Wishing Wings here, too? And these other humans?"

"You were under an enchantment that tried to keep you from earning your magic," said Sky Dance. "They all helped get you caught and set free before sunset."

"An enchantment!" exclaimed Blue Rain. "Oh, my! I don't even remember coming out of my chrysalis. I hope I didn't say or do anything I might regret."

Addie, Clara, Sky Dance, and Shimmer Leaf all laughed. Maybe someday Blue Rain would hear the whole story, but this wasn't quite the right time.

"Hey, guys!" shouted a voice. Addie turned to see Oliver running out of the house, a phone in his hand. "My brother's coming home for a visit! He'll be here next week!"

"Yay!" called Addie.

"Can we meet him?" asked Clara.

"Of course! When I told him I had two new friends next door, he was so happy!"

Oliver ran back inside with the phone.

Sky Dance turned to Blue Rain. "Nice work. Especially for a beginner!"

"Thanks," said Blue Rain.

"We shall all return to Wishing Wing Grove and celebrate," said Rose Glow, and all the other butterflies chattered enthusiastically.

"We'll see you tomorrow, I bet," said Sky Dance to Addie as the butterflies began to take to the air.

"One more New Bloom to save," said Addie.

"We're pros by now," added Clara. "This one will be a breeze."

Would it?

As Addie watched the sky fill with every fluttering color she'd ever imagined, her heart swelled with wonder and pride. She'd seen and done things in the past few days that she'd never imagined possible. Whatever happened tomorrow, she was ready. She was ready for anything!

Turn the page for a glimpse at Addie and Clara's next magical butterfly adventure!

Addie is so excited to get a special visitor for the weekend, but things don't go quite as planned. Meanwhile, a new butterfly, Spring Shine, has come out of her chrysalis and somehow believes she's missing her magic—even though there's nothing wrong with her at all! When Spring Shine disappears, Addie must find her, and figure out a way to raise her spirits. Will she be able to help her friend, and discover who's responsible for this mess, before another butterfly gets hurt?

Available now!

A brown cardboard box sat in the corner of Addie Gibson's bedroom, looking lonely and forgotten. The words DESK STUFF were written in red marker across the top.

Addie had been staring at this box all morning. It was the last one she needed to unpack since her family had moved from the city to a house in the country.

But she was having trouble doing it. The box was filled with things she'd need for her new school, which would be starting in a couple of weeks. Thinking about her new school gave Addie an instant, nervous lump in her throat. Opening the box meant it would all be way too real, way too soon.

"Okay," she said to the box. "Enough is enough. Let's do this."

The box seemed okay with that.

Addie dragged it into the middle of the room, sat down on the floor, tore open the packing tape, and reached her hand inside.

First, she found a stationery set decorated with her initials. Next, a case of colored pens and some erasers shaped like cupcakes. Then, a notebook with an adorable baby bunny on the cover, and an old cookie tin filled with tape, scissors, and glue. Finally, Addie's fingers found the sharp corners of what might be a book. When she pulled it out, she gasped in surprise.

Her old diary!

It was the fancy kind, a hardcover with thick, blank pages that smelled a little like flowers and a little like a library. Addie flipped through it, recognizing her own neat handwriting in blue pen. She used to write in the diary every night, right before bed. She'd loved recording the events of each day and the feelings that went along with them. But halfway through the book, the handwriting ended; all the pages after that were empty.

Addie knew exactly when she'd stopped writing in the diary. It was the night her parents told her they would be

moving to a place called Brook Forest, hours away from everything she'd ever known and especially from her best friend, Violet. Addie had been so upset, she'd cried on and off for days. Why would she want to remember that kind of sadness?

But those feelings were fading fast. Her first week in Brook Forest had been filled with the most amazing and wonderful happenings. Those events belonged in her diary! Addie grabbed a pen from the case, turned to the first blank page, and began to write.

Dear Diary, Guess what? In the woods behind our new house, there's a place called Wishing Wing Grove. It's the home of the Wishing Wing butterflies, who can make magic by turning one thing into another. My butterfly BFF is named Sky Dance. She's basically a princess because her mother is the queen, Rose Glow. Clara also has a butterfly BFF: Sky Dance's sister Shimmer Leaf. They came to us for help because there's a dark enchantment on a group of New Blooms, which are Wishing Wings that have just changed from caterpillars to butterflies. So far we've broken the enchantment on three butterflies and helped them earn their magic: Shimmer Leaf, Tiger Streak, and Blue Rain. There's one more left, but we still haven't figured out who cast the enchantment and caused all this trouble in the first place.

Addie stopped and read what she wrote. Did it sound crazy? Well, yes. Of course. But so what? This was for her eyes only. It felt great to begin telling the story of her new life.

Addie shifted the diary in her lap, and a photo fell out from between two pages. When she picked it up, she recognized it instantly: a snapshot of herself and Violet at a school Halloween party. Violet was dressed as a half-angel, half-devil; Addie was Dorothy from *The Wizard of Oz*. The memory of that party, and all the other fun times with Violet, flooded her with a happy-sad feeling. She had already made new friends in Brook Forest, but Violet would always be special. Addie ran her fingers over the gold bracelet on her wrist. When she'd first met Sky Dance and made a wish to stay close to Violet forever, the butterfly had made the bracelet for her. The bracelet was filled with magic that would keep the girls' friendship strong.

"Are you missing Violet?" asked a high, musical voice.

Addie looked up to see a very familiar pair of butterfly wings on her window sill. They were pink and turquoise, with cloud patterns on them.

"Sky Dance!" Addie exclaimed. "Please come in!"

Sky Dance fluttered into the room and flew a slow loop around it before landing on Addie's bedpost. "So this is your hollow," she said with an approving nod of her furry pink head. "I like it!"

"Thanks," Addie said. "It's no Wishing Wing Grove, but it's cozy. Are you here because the last New Bloom has come out?"

"Actually," Sky Dance began with a sigh, "I'm here because she *hasn't* come out. We've all been waiting and waiting! Everyone's afraid that Spring Shine— that's her name —won't emerge at all. It's really stressful. I decided to visit you instead."

"That does sound nerve-racking," agreed Addie. "I'm glad you came."

"I'm worried, Addie. Even if we

can break Spring Shine's enchantment like we did for Shimmer Leaf, Tiger Streak, and Blue Rain, we still don't know who cast it in the first place. The next set of New Blooms could be in danger the same way."

"I know," Addie said. "I was thinking about that, too. Let's focus on making sure Spring Shine's okay. Then we can try to solve this mystery."

There was a sudden, loud *rap rap rap* on Addie's door. Addie's heart leaped; if it was her mother, she'd have to hide Sky Dance. Maybe the butterfly could pretend to be one of the glass animal figurines on Addie's bookshelf.

"Addie, who are you talking to?" asked Clara's voice.

Phew, thought Addie. "Come in and you'll see," she replied.

Clara burst in, holding her new kitten, Squish (who used to be a stuffed toy kitten, before Wishing Wing magic made him real). When Clara spotted Sky Dance, she smiled. "Oh, good. You're both here! Shimmer Leaf just sent me a thought message that Spring Shine's chrysalis is starting to open!"

Because Shimmer Leaf was Clara's Wishing Wing, they could send messages to each other with their thoughts. Addie and Sky Dance could do the same.

Sky Dance sailed excitedly into the air and flew a figure eight. "Let's go! I'll meet you outside!"

Jennifer Castle is the author of the Butterfly Wishes series and many other books for children and teens, including *Famous Friends* and *Together at Midnight*. She lives in New York's Hudson Valley with her husband, two daughters, and two striped cats, at the edge of a deep wood that is most definitely filled with magic—she just hasn't found it yet.

www.jennifercastle.com

Tracy Bishop is the illustrator of the Butterfly Wishes series. She has loved drawing magical creatures like fairies, unicorns, and dragons since she was little and is thrilled to get to draw magical butterflies. She lives in the San Francisco Bay Area with her husband, son, and a hairy dog named Harry.

www.tracybishop.com

Unicorn Princesses BY EMILY BLISS

Welcome to an enchanted land ruled by unicorn princesses!

COMING SOON!

www.bloomsbury.com
Facebook: KidsBloomsbury
Twitter: BloomsburyKids

Princess Ponies

BY CHLOE RYDER

Don't miss Pippa's journey to find the golden horseshoes and save Chevalia!

www.bloomsbury.com
Facebook: KidsBloomsbury
Twitter: BloomsburyKids